Y0-ARG-188

Eddie fired again . . .

"If you keep shooting at rocks, you're going to run out of bullets yourself," Win said easily.

Startled, Eddie turned around. The expression in his face reflected the shock of seeing Win, not only in a place totally different from where Eddie thought he was, but also because Win was naked, except for a pair of underbriefs.

"What the hell?" Eddie shouted, swinging his rifle around while, at the same time, jacking in a new round.

Eddie got the lever down, but he never pulled it back up. Win's right arm whipped forward and the knife flashed once in the sun as it sped across the distance between the two men. It buried itself to the hilt in Eddie's chest, penetrating his heart and killing him even before he could fully realize what was happening to him . . .

DON'T MISS THESE
ALL-ACTION WESTERN SERIES
FROM THE BERKLEY PUBLISHING GROUP

THE GUNSMITH by J. R. Roberts
Clint Adams was a legend among lawmen, outlaws, and ladies. They called him . . . the Gunsmith.

LONGARM by Tabor Evans
The popular long-running series about U.S. Deputy Marshal Long—his life, his loves, his fight for justice.

SLOCUM by Jake Logan
Today's longest-running action Western. John Slocum rides a deadly trail of hot blood and cold steel.

BUSHWHACKERS by B. J. Lanagan
An action-packed series by the creators of Longarm! The rousing adventures of the most brutal gang of cutthroats ever assembled—Quantrill's Raiders.

BUSHWHACKERS

A TIME FOR KILLING

B. J. Lanagan

JOVE BOOKS, NEW YORK

If you purchased this book without a cover, you should be aware that
this book is stolen property. It was reported as "unsold and destroyed"
to the publisher, and neither the author nor the publisher has received
any payment for this "stripped book."

A TIME FOR KILLING

A Jove Book / published by arrangement with
the author

PRINTING HISTORY
Jove edition / June 1999

All rights reserved.
Copyright © 1999 by Penguin Putnam Inc.
This book may not be reproduced in whole or in part,
by mimeograph or any other means, without permission.
For information address: The Berkley Publishing Group,
a division of Penguin Putnam Inc.,
375 Hudson Street, New York, New York 10014.

The Penguin Putnam Inc. World Wide Web site address is
http://www.penguinputnam.com

ISBN: 0-515-12574-1

A JOVE BOOK®
Jove Books are published by The Berkley Publishing Group,
a division of Penguin Putnam Inc.,
375 Hudson Street, New York, New York 10014.
JOVE and the "J" design
are trademarks belonging to Penguin Putnam Inc.

PRINTED IN THE UNITED STATES OF AMERICA

10 9 8 7 6 5 4 3 2 1

Chapter 1

IT WAS FIFTEEN YEARS NOW, SINCE WIN AND JOE COULTER had left Missouri. During the Civil War the two brothers rode with the Confederate raiders, William C. Quantrill and Bloody Bill Anderson. Those who fought under their black flag were called Bushwhackers, and they had fought a war within a war against men from Kansas, who were called Jayhawkers.

On the grand scheme of things, the skirmishes fought between the Bushwhackers and the Jayhawkers didn't amount to much. Names like Prairie Lick, Gomer's Crossing, and Dumey's Farm, didn't resonate like Shiloh, Gettysburg, or Antietam. But a comparison of the number of men engaged show the battles between Missourians and Kansans to be among the bloodiest of the war. This almost private war took on a personal aspect that had little to do with honor and much to do with killing.

After the war was over the soldiers of the two regular armies came home, some in victory, some in defeat, but all in honor. Neighbor who had fought against neighbor put down the gun and picked up the plow. They resumed the lives they had abandoned when they marched off under the flag of their cause.

That was not the case with the Bushwhackers. They

weren't allowed to enjoy the peace. Men who had ridden with Quantrill and Anderson were branded thieves and murderers. Rewards were posted for their capture, in many cases dead or alive. Most had no recourse but to leave Missouri.

What made it particularly unfair was that the Jayhawkers, who had been every bit as bloody as the Bushwhackers, did not suffer that same fate. They had been on the winning side. As a result, their crimes were considered acts of war, and to them went the spoils of victory. For when a bushwhacker had to sell his farm at distress prices, or give it up for taxes, it often wound up in the hands of someone who had been their bitterest enemy.

Some, like the James boys and the Youngers and Daltons, believed they had no choice but to take up the outlaw trail. Others who rode with Quantrill left Missouri to start a new life. Win and Joe Coulter were among that lot. Another such man was Jeb Pemberton.

As Jeb sat at the kitchen table of his west Texas ranch, he contemplated the events of the previous fifteen years that had brought him to the present. Things were fine for him now, but it had been a long struggle to reach this point.

He had been a sergeant in Win and Joe's company of bushwhackers, and when he returned from the war, he found that his farm had been confiscated for taxes and his wife and two small children were turned out to fend for themselves. With money borrowed from relatives, Jeb bought a wagon and moved his family to Texas.

There, by hard work and perseverance, Jeb had prospered. His small ranch was thriving, and as his son got older and was able to help, it grew even larger. It had turned out to be a good life.

Jeb finished his cup of coffee and looked across the table at the woman he had married, twenty years before. Mary was sitting on the other side of the table, hulling peas.

"Well, tomorrow is the big day," Jeb said. "The Fourth of July picnic. Are you ready for it?"

"Well, now, just why do you think I've been shelling all these peas?" she replied. "You don't think we could eat this much by ourselves, do you?"

Jeb laughed. "I don't know. Eddie's got a pretty big appetite."

"He gets it from his father," Mary said, as she stripped open a hull, dumped the peas into a bowl, then discarded that hull and reached for another one.

Jeb picked up a handful of peas and began shelling them.

"You don't have to do that," Mary said. "It's woman's work."

"I eat 'em, don't I?" Jeb said. "Won't hurt me to shell a few."

Mary reached over to put her hand on her husband's hand. "You're a good man," she said.

"It'll be good to see Win and Joe again, don't you think?" Jeb asked. He was referring to the letter they had received a few days earlier, in which Win Coulter had said that he and Joe would be passing through on the fourth.

"I don't know, Jeb," Mary said. "I've been worryin' some about that. To be truthful with you, I'd just as soon they not come."

Jeb stared at Mary. "Why, Mary Pemberton, how can you say such a thing? They're home folks. Fact is, they are the only ones from home we've seen in all the time we've lived out here."

"I know, and when the children were younger, it never bothered me. But Eddie is at that age now. I'm worried about the kind of influence Win and Joe will have on him. He thinks they are heroes."

"In my mind, they *are* heroes."

"But, you know what kind of life they live. There's no telling how many men they've killed."

"That may be so," Jeb said, "but I'd wager they've never killed anyone who didn't need killing."

"It's for God to determine who needs killing, not man," Mary said.

"They've been here several times, and they've always been the perfect gentlemen. Anyway, why am I having to defend them to you? They're your cousins, not mine."

"We're not that close of kin. Their mother was my mother's first cousin, that's all," Mary said. She sighed. "But you're right, they have always been well behaved around us. And it will be good to see Missouri folk again."

"Do you miss Missouri that much, Mary?"

Mary got a pensive look, then brushed a fall of hair away from her face. "I reckon I miss the hills some," she admitted. "I like the way the fog hangs in the notches in the mornin'. I like listening to the frogs at night. And I like to see green. Everything out here is so brown."

"Maybe some day, I can take you home again," Jeb said.

Mary smiled, and squeezed Jeb's hand. "Don't be foolish," she said. "We *are* home. I've got my man, my children. What more would a woman want?"

"The day you said you'd marry me was the luckiest day of my life," Jeb said.

Together, husband and wife finished shelling the peas. Then, when the last of them was finished, Mary put a cloth over the bowl, then stood up and stretched. "I'd better get to bed. I'm going to have to start frying chicken awfully early in the morning to get enough done for the picnic."

South of the Pemberton ranch by about one hour's ride, two men sat around a campfire, watching the flames lick up around the bottom of a blue metal coffeepot. Julio Mendoza was only half Mexican, but with his long, sweeping mustache, wide sombrero, and colorful serape he wore, the casual observer would be hard-pressed to find any Anglo in him until they heard him talk. He spoke both Spanish and English with equal ease.

"I don't see why we couldn't have stayed in town tonight," Mendoza said. "Rosa was going to spend the night with me."

Charley Beckett snorted. "And what were you going to do for money?" he asked.

"I don't need any money for Rosa," Mendoza said. "Rosa likes me."

"Rosa likes anyone who'll spread her legs," Beckett said. "Get a little money in your pocket, and you can have anyone you want."

Beckett was ten years older than Mendoza. He had a long, purple lightning-flash of a scar running through his left eye, down across his cheek, and hooking up just under his mouth, the result of a wartime encounter with a saber-wielding, Confederate cavalry officer.

"And the rancher you told me about has money?" Mendoza asked.

"Lots of money," Beckett insisted. "I've heard them talk about him. He is one of the most successful ranchers around."

"Maybe he doesn't keep it with him."

"He's got it, all right," Beckett insisted. "He rode with Quantrill. They robbed so many banks during the war, that people who rode with him don't trust them anymore. He probably has it all stuffed down inside a sock and hidden in his mattress. It'll be like taking candy from a baby." Beckett laughed and snorted. "By God, it'll be good taking money from his damn rebel hide."

"The war has been over for many years now," Mendoza said.

"Not for me, it ain't," Beckett said. "I hate ever' rebel bastard what ever forked a horse. And I reckon they all hate me."

In a small, West Texas town some seven hours farther south, Win, and Joe Coulter had decided to treat themselves to a night in a hotel. They ate a good supper, then took two rooms on the second floor, overlooking the street.

Before going up to their rooms, a brief business transaction took place between them and two of the more attractive soiled doves who plied their avocation in that particular hotel. It was not the first time the brothers had been there . . . and this wasn't the first time they had come to an arrangement with these two girls. Thus, negotiations between them passed rather quickly.

When the business of money was taken care of, the boys retired to their respective rooms, accompanied by the young woman of their choice.

Win had chosen Virginia Ann Lucas, and she was now completely, gloriously, and beautifully naked. She was in bed, sitting astraddle Win's legs. She didn't take him into her right away, but wrapped her hands around his erection instead. When she did so, her fingers managed to feel hot and cold at the same time.

From his perspective on his back, Win's view of Virginia Ann was somewhat blocked by the condition of his obvious arousal. Her small, but well-formed breasts were clearly visible though, along with the erect nipples.

"This is the part of my job I like best," Virginia Ann said. She squeezed him. "I like it when I am holding the power in my hands."

"I hope you are going to do more than hold it in your hands," Win said.

"Oh . . . I'll think of something more to do," Virginia Ann replied. She leaned forward until her breasts were but a breath away from Win's mouth. Twisting her body, she brought one of the nipples into contact with his lips.

As Win nibbled and sucked her nipples, she twisted her body from side to side so that each of them got equal attention.

"You aren't the only one who can do that, you know," Virginia Ann said.

"What do you mean?"

"Shall I show you?"

She changed positions so that she could take his shaft

into her mouth. With a grunt of pleasure, Win put his hands on the back of her head, running his fingers through her hair as she began using her mouth, working her jaws in and out, decreasing and increasing the pressure by sucking, and, most stimulating of all, by using her tongue to flick, caress, and tease him.

Even as Virginia Ann was working on him, Win could hear a thumping sound against the wall from the room next door. The thumping was augmented by the rhythmic squeak of bedsprings.

The occupant of that room was Win's brother, Joe, and it was he who was responsible for the thumping and squeaking. He couldn't help it. Joe was a good sized man, and if a bedstead was not quite solid enough, and the bedsprings were loose, and he was actively engaged with a willing female partner, as he was at this precise moment, then some noise was inevitable.

But the bed wasn't the only thing making noise. Joe was driving into Linda with long, sensory-invoking thrusts, and she simply couldn't hold back.

"Oh, yes!" Linda squealed in orgiastic delight. "Oh, yes, it's wonderful! Yes, yes, yes!"

As Joe maintained a steady pace of hard, quick, piston-like drives, Linda's words ran together into a sound that burst from her throat in one long sob. She writhed and moaned, keeping her eyes shut while she shuddered in spasms of ecstasy.

When it was all over, some ten minutes later, Win heard the doors close as Virginia Ann and Linda met in the hall. There, they began giggling and comparing notes. There was some basis for comparison, for on their previous visit to this hotel, Linda had been with Win and Virginia Ann, with Joe.

As Joe was fond of saying, it had all come full circle.

Chapter 2

EARLY THE NEXT MORNING AT THE PEMBERTON RANCH, fifteen-year-old Emma Pemberton was listening to the milk squirting into the bucket as she squeezed the cow's teats. She had already gathered the eggs, and the chickens were now wandering around the yard, clucking contentedly and pecking at the ground-up corn she had scattered for them.

Today was the Fourth of July, and the whole family was going into town for the celebration. There would be a picnic at noon—her mother had been frying chicken since before sun-up—then games all afternoon. Her father and brother were entered in the team horseshoe pitching contest. They won last year and had been practicing for a month to defend their championship.

Emma's mother was entering her special plum jelly in the jams and jelly contest, and Emma had worked for a full year on a quilt.

That was all fun, but the thing Emma was most looking forward to was the barn dance to be held tonight. Last week she heard that the chamber of commerce had hired a real band all the way from St. Louis to provide the music. She hoped that was true. Mr. Tidwell and the Beamer brothers, who normally supplied the music, were all right. But they were old, and didn't know any of the latest songs. It would be nice to have up-to-date music to dance to.

Her brother, Eddie, seemed more excited about cousins Win and Joe coming than he was about celebrating the Fourth.

"Ain't it wonderful, us bein' kin to the Coulters?" Eddie had asked over and over. "Why, they've killed more men than anybody!"

Emma said that scarcely seemed reason to make a hero of someone, but Eddie's enthusiasm wasn't dampened.

She heard the pump handle working and, looking around, saw her brother. He was holding his head under the mouth of the pump while he worked the handle. Ice-cold, deep-well water cascaded over him, washing away the dirt and sweat from his morning chores. Walking quietly, Emma stepped up to the pump and jerked away the towel, just as Eddie reached for it.

"Emma!" Eddie said angrily. "Gimme the towel you took."

"What towel?"

"If you don't want me to dry my face on your dress, you'll give me the towel."

"Oh, you mean this towel?" Emma said. She handed the towel to him.

"Very funny," Eddie said. He took the towel then began drying his face.

"Eddie, Papa won't let me ride home from the picnic with Tommy Anders. He says I'm too young."

"You are too young."

"I'm only one year younger than you are," Emma protested.

"That don't make no difference. You're a girl."

"I'm not a girl. I'm a woman, near 'bout," Emma said. She leaned against the split-rail fence and thrust her hip out, proudly displaying the developing curves of her young body. "You tell Papa to let me ride home from the picnic with Tommy. Papa will listen to you."

"Ha! In a pig's eye he will," Eddie said. "You know

Pa doesn't listen to anyone.'' He lay the towel back across the rail. "Come on, let's go get breakfast. I'm starved.''

"All we're goin' to have is biscuits and some chicken gravy,'' Emma said. "Mama's been frying chicken all morning.''

"That's good enough for me,'' Eddie said.

Brother and sister walked back up the path to the house, following the aroma of fried chicken. Eddie pushed the door open, then came to a complete halt, his eyes wide with confusion. His mother and father were both in the middle of the floor, tied to kitchen chairs. They tried to shout warnings but their shouts came out as squeaks because both were gagged.

"Ma! Pa!" Eddie shouted, starting toward his father.

"That's far enough, boy," a voice said. Two armed men stepped out of the pantry. One had a long, purple scar running through his left eye, down across his cheek, and hooking up just under his mouth. The other was medium-sized and dark complexioned, with a long mustache. Both were eating chicken.

"I know who you are. You're Kansas Charley Beckett!" Eddie gasped, recognizing the man with the scar.

"What about that, Charley? The boy knows your name." The one with the mustache said.

"That don't matter none," Charley said. "The boy ain't needed.''

Charley pointed his gun at Eddie and pulled the trigger. The gun roared. A wicked flash of flame jumped from the barrel and a cloud of smoke billowed out over the table. The bullet hit Eddie in the forehead, then burst out from the back of his head, carrying with it bits of bone, skin, and brain matter. Heavy drops of blood splattered from Eddie's wound onto Emma's face and fanned out onto the bodice of her dress.

"Eddie!" Emma screamed, as her brother, already dead, fell to the floor. She dropped to her knees beside him and put her hands on his face, trying desperately to deny what she was seeing with her eyes.

Suddenly Jeb managed to work himself free from the ropes, and he jumped up from his chair. His move was so quick and unexpected, that he caught Beckett by surprise. Jeb knocked him back and began wrestling with him for the gun.

"Mendoza! Get this son of a bitch off me!" Beckett screamed.

Moving quickly, Mendoza stepped over to the two struggling men. He stuck his gun into Jeb's side, then, at point-blank range, pulled the trigger. As Jeb was going down, Mendoza and then Beckett shot him again.

"We shouldn't of killed the son of a bitch," Mendoza said. "Now, we'll never learn where he keeps his money."

"We'll ask her."

Beckett removed Mary's gag. She had just seen her son and husband murdered before her eyes and was in a state of shock.

"Where's the money?" Beckett asked.

"Money? What money?" Mary replied in a confused voice. "I don't know what money you are talking about."

"Don't lie to me, woman. A ranch like this? You've got to have money around, somewhere."

"We keep our money in the bank."

"You're lying!" Beckett said. He slapped her.

"No!" Emma shouted. "Don't hit her again. I'll show you where the money is."

"Emma, what are you talking about? There is no money except the money that's in the bank."

"What about the money papa buried under the tree, at the south end of the ranch?" Emma asked.

"The south end of the ranch?" Mary replied, her voice showing her confusion.

"You know, the money he buried when cousins Win and Joe were here?"

Mary realized then what Emma had in mind. She was

going to lead the two men south, in the direction from which Win and Joe Coulter would be coming. She was taking a chance that Win and Joe would be coming at just the right moment. But no . . . that was too big a chance. They probably wouldn't get here until mid afternoon.

"Emma, no, don't do this," Mary said.

"Take care of her," Beckett growled, and Mendoza raised his gun and cocked it.

"No!" Emma shouted. "If you hurt her, I'll never tell you where the money is. Leave her alone."

Mendoza looked over at Beckett. Beckett thought about it for a moment, then motioned with his hand. "All right, leave her be," he said. He looked at Emma. "But girl, you better come up with that money, fast."

Chapter 3

EMMA HAD NO WAY OF KNOWING THAT WIN AND JOE Coulter were still twenty miles away at that moment. They had stopped at a stagecoach way station to buy themselves a meal, feed and water their mounts, and fill their canteens.

"Did you tell Virginia Ann that we would be back next week?" Joe asked, as he forked up a large bite of biscuit and gravy.

"No," Win said. "Why?"

"Linda insisted that you told her that."

Win laughed. "That's just Linda talking. She's trying to get you to come back, that's all," he said as he began rolling a cigarette.

"Yeah, that's what I figured. You want the rest of that biscuit?" Joe asked, pointing to the half-eaten biscuit remaining on Win's plate.

Win handed the biscuit to his brother. "I wouldn't think of depriving you."

"Well, I mean, if you don't want it," Joe said.

"You better save some room for the food at the picnic tonight," Win said. "I'll bet Mary is making a couple of her cherry pies. And you know she's frying chicken."

"Yeah, she does fry some good chicken," Joe said.

"Too bad I didn't think about marrying her before Jeb did."

"She's our cousin, for crying out loud. How could you marry her?"

"She's not 'ny closer kin to us than Zee is to Jesse, and they got married."

"Yeah, well, if you ask me, I always did think Jesse James was a little touched in the head."

The proprietor called to them from behind the counter. "You boys want 'ny more coffee? No charge for it, I need to get rid of this, 'cause I'm 'bout to make some fresh."

"Yeah, thanks," Win said. He took his and Joe's cups over to the counter. As the coffee was being poured, he happened to see a folded-up newspaper lying there. A name on the front page caught his eye, and he reached for it.

"This paper for sale?"

"Somebody left it," the proprietor said. "You can have it, if you want. It's a couple of weeks old."

Win nodded his appreciation, then returned to the table. He handed one of the cups of coffee to Joe.

"What's got you so interested?" Joe asked, taking a sip.

"This paper says Kansas Charley Beckett's been seen in the area."

"That's right," the proprietor said, overhearing them. "They say he's been seen two or three times."

"The sonofabitch rode with Emil Slaughter, didn't he?" Joe asked.

"That he did, little brother. That he did."

It was 1861. Win and Joe Coulter, who were just returning home from a business trip for their father, stopped at the gate that led onto the Coulter farm and looked at the sign:

COULTER FARM
ESTABLISHED, 1835
"THE TRUTH IS, ALL MIGHT BE FREE IF THEY VALUED

FREEDOM AND DEFENDED IT AS THEY OUGHT.''
SAMUEL ADAMS

A grasshopper was clinging to the faded lettering and a clump of weeds had grown up in front of the sign. Win dismounted and pulled the weeds so that the sign was clearly visible.

"I thought Pa told you to re-paint this sign," Win said.

"I thought he told you."

Win tossed the weed aside, then brushed the dirt off his hands. He tilted his head to one side and squinted. "It's not all that bad, is it? I mean, you can still read it."

"I can read it," Joe said. "Course, I could read it even if the words weren't there. Pa used to bring me out here and read it to me. It's the first thing I ever learned to read."

Win laughed as he remounted. "You weren't reading it, little brother, you were memorizing it."

The two brothers rode through the gate and started up the long road. Although they were back on their own farm, they wouldn't be able to actually see the house until they topped the hill. Their horses frightened a rabbit, which bounded down the lane in front of them for several feet before darting off into the safety of the tall grass.

Joe sniffed the air. "Pa must've been burnin' some brush. I can smell it."

"Yeah," Win agreed. "I can smell it, too."

They reached the crest of the hill then and looked down where the house, barn, and other outbuildings should be. But there were no buildings there. Instead there were several blackened piles of burned-out rubble . . . all that remained of what had been the barn, smokehouse, outhouse, and house. Two lonely brick chimneys marked each end of what had been the house and, from the charred skeletal remains, wisps of smoke still curled up into the bright blue sky.

• • •

Their farm had been burned, their father murdered, and their mother, murdered, and raped by a gang of cutthroats riding for Emil Slaughter under the banner of the Jayhawkers. It had been that incident that set the brothers to riding for Quantrill. Over the course of the war, they caught up, not only with Slaughter, but with the specific individuals who had killed their father and raped and killed their mother. The boys had extracted their retribution.

Since the war they had learned the names of every man who had ridden with Slaughter on that night. Most were dead, but some were still alive. Kansas Charley Beckett was one of them.

"Joe? You all right?" Win asked.

Joe blinked, coming back from his memories. "Yeah," Joe said. "Yeah, I'm all right. But I'm going to be more than all right when we finally catch up with that son of a bitch."

They were four hours from the way station. As they rode across the open range, the metal bits jangled against the horses' teeth, the horses' hooves clattered on the hard rock, and the leather saddles creaked beneath them.

Their boots were dusty and well worn, the metal of their spurs, dull with time. Both men wore Colt .44s at their hips and carried Winchester .44-40s in their saddle sheaths.

"Damn, I didn't remember Jeb's place being this far," Joe said.

Win chuckled. "You say this every time we come."

"Well, hell, it's true, every time," Joe replied. He saw something out of the corner of his eye, then turned in his saddle for a better look.

"Win," he said. "Take a look." He nodded toward the mesa.

Win looked in the direction Joe had indicated. There, circling in the sky, were several buzzards.

"Something's dying," Win said.

"Or already dead."

"Rabbit? Coyote?" Win suggested.

Joe shook his head. "Don't think so. I think it's bigger'n that."

"We'd better check it out."

The girl's nude body was blackened and swollen in the sun. She had stab wounds all over her body and one of her breasts had been hacked away. It was as brutal and sense-less a murder as either of the brothers had ever encountered, and during the war they had seen more than their share of brutal killings.

"My God," Win said. "That's Jeb's girl! That's Emma."

The two brothers dismounted and studied not only the corpse, but the ground around it.

"We're in luck here," Joe said, pointing to the ground. "There are two of them, and one of the horses is wearing a crooked shoe. See how the end turns in, there?"

"Yeah," Win said. He looked toward the distant western horizon, in the direction the riders had gone. "I wish we could start out after them now."

"Why can't we? We need to get on them, before the trail gets cold."

Win shook his head. "No. We need to get this girl back to her mama and daddy. Besides, if it doesn't rain, the trail will still be here.

It was a solemn Fourth of July celebration, followed the next day by a even more solemn funeral for Jeb, Eddie, and Emma Pemberton. Mary was able to identify the two men as Kansas Charley Beckett and Julio Mendoza, and the sheriff called for a posse to help him bring the killers in.

"Did you boys see any sign, anything that would give us a lead?" the sheriff asked Win and Joe.

"Not a thing," Win replied. "The ground was like solid rock. No telling which way they went."

Joe looked at Win in surprise, but didn't say anything.

"You boys going to join the posse tomorrow?" the sheriff asked. "I reckon you will be, seein' as you were friends of Jeb."

"If you don't mind, Sheriff, I think my brother and I could be more help by going out on our own to see if we can pick up a trail. If we find anything, we'll get back to you."

The sheriff stroked his chin for a moment or two. It was obvious he didn't quite believe Win. Then he went over to his desk and opened the drawer. He pulled out a couple of badges and handed them to Joe and Win.

"I don't know what you boys have in mind," he said. "But maybe I should make you my deputies. Most the other counties in Texas will recognize them . . . it'll give you some authority . . . not much, but maybe just enough to keep you out of trouble."

"Thanks," Win said. He took the badge, but he didn't pin it on. Instead, he dropped it into his shirt pocket. Joe did the same.

"Remember," the sheriff said as they left his office. "If you find anything . . . get word back to the posse."

"How will we find the posse?" Win asked.

"If you had a gut feeling for where Beckett and Mendoza were headed for, what would that be?" the sheriff asked.

Win paused for a moment. "I'd say they were headed west." He knew that was exactly where they were going, but he didn't want company when he and Joe started after them. He knew, also, that the sheriff knew he didn't want company, so he was taking a chance that the sheriff wouldn't believe him.

"You think they are headed west, do you?"

"That's what I think," Win said.

The sheriff stared at Win, then he smiled. "Well, I'll tell you what. I know that you an' your brother want to go off on your own, so I'm figurin', there's no way you're goin' to tell me the truth. So, I got me a gut feeling of my own. And my gut feeling says they headed south.''

"Could be they went that way,'' Win agreed.

The sheriff laughed. "You got to be pretty quick to put one over on me.'' He looked out the front window at the group of men who were beginning to drift over to sign up for the posse. There were cowboys, dray men, a couple of farmers, and more than one bar-fly, signing on for the dollar per day they would get when it was all over. "Hell, the truth is, I can't blame you,'' he added. "If I didn't have to, there's no way on God's green earth I would take this bunch of outcasts and rabble with me.'' He looked back at Win and Joe. "Good luck, boys,'' he said.

Win and Joe had crossed into New Mexico the day before. This wasn't new ground for them. They had been in this part of the country several times over the last couple of years, and actually knew it quite well. It was a pleasant surprise to them when they realized that Beckett was leading them this way.

Joe stopped, then dismounted and unhooked his canteen. He took a swallow, then poured some water into his hat and held it in front of his horse. The horse drank thirstily, though the small amount of water did little to slake the animal's thirst. The horse began nuzzling Joe for more.

"That little dab of water didn't do anything but make it worse for the poor critter,'' Win said.

"You're probably right,'' Joe answered quietly. "But I had to do something. I can't stand to see him suffer so.''

"We'll reach the monastery before nightfall, and there will be water there.''

"Yeah. And it'll be good to see Padre Dominick again,'' Joe said. "I'm anxious for a rematch at checkers. I've got a couple of moves in mind that he won't catch on to.''

Win laughed. "As I recall, that's what you said last time we were through here, and he beat you pretty good.''

"Yeah, he did, didn't he? I'm glad he's a religious sort of guy and doesn't bet on his games. If he did, my horse wouldn't be thirsty now, 'cause the good padre would own it."

Chapter 4

THE MONASTERY THEY WERE DISCUSSING STOOD ALONE IN the desert, a testament to the faith that God would provide for the righteous, even in conditions as harsh as this. According to records kept on file in the monastery, it had been built by the Spanish nearly two hundred years earlier. There were no natural sources of food or water. The monastery garden was supported by irrigation, the water for which was brought in by the barrelful in small, mule-drawn carts, from a not always dependable river, twelve miles to the East.

Except for the religious order which lived in the monastery, no one, Indian, Mexican, or American, lived within fifty miles of the place. As far as anyone could tell, no one had ever lived there. The question was why had the monastery been built there in the first place? And why did the religious order continue to occupy it?

The last time Win and Joe were through there, Win had posed that same question to Father Dominick. With a small smile, Father Dominick had replied, "The answer is a mystery, and the mystery is the answer."

Win finally came to the conclusion that the monastery was there for no other purpose than to provide rest and water for the traveler. Anyone coming this way would have to stop at the monastery, for there was no other source of food or water within several miles in any direction.

He also realized that Beckett must know that, for, why else would his trail have led them there?

They reached the monastery just before dark. The abbey was surrounded by high stone walls and secured by a heavy oak gate. Joe pulled on a rope that was attached to a short section of log. The log swung away, then fell back, banging against the large, heavy gates with a booming thunder that resonated through the entire monastery. A moment later a small window slid open and a brown-hooded face appeared in the opening.

"Who are you?" the face asked.

For just a second, Win was confused. The face in the window belonged to Brother Tobias, and Win knew that Tobias knew them. Yet, Tobias was clearly acting as if he didn't.

"My name is Win Coulter. This is my brother, Joe."

"What do you want?"

"We are weary travelers. We want food, water, and shelter. Can't we come in?"

"I'm sorry. We can grant no entry."

"But, Brother, we are out of water. You can not turn us away."

"I am truly sorry," the monk said. "God go with you." The little window slammed shut.

There was no way Tobias wouldn't have recognized them, so, from the moment Brother Tobias asked who they were, Win knew that something was wrong. That was why he didn't insist that they were known. Brother Tobias was trying to send them a message. The message had to be that Beckett and Mendoza were there.

Charley Beckett and Julio Mendoza had been standing just inside the gate when Win called. Mendoza was peering through the crack, between the timbers of the gate.

"What are they doin' now?" Beckett asked.

"They ain't doin' nothin', 'cept just ridin' off," Mendoza answered.

Beckett chuckled, then put his pistol away. He looked at the short, overweight monk. "You done that real good, Padre," he said. "I don't think they suspect a thing."

"I am not a priest," Brother Tobias replied. "Therefore I am not addressed as Father."

"Yeah, well, brother, sister, father, padre, reverend, pastor, what the hell difference does it make? All you religious guys are called somethin'. Come on, let's go see if the cook has our supper finished. I'm starvin'."

The three men walked back across the little courtyard, which, because of the irrigation and loving care bestowed upon it by the brothers of the order, was lush with flowers, fruit trees, and a vegetable garden. There were a dozen or more monks in the yard, each occupied by some specific task.

The building they entered was surprisingly cool, kept that way by the hanging ollas, which, while sacrificing some of the precious water by evaporation, paid off the investment by lowering the temperature by several degrees.

"Who was at the gate?" Father Dominick asked.

"Strangers, Father. I do not know who they were," Brother Tobias said. "They asked for food and water."

"And you denied them sanctuary?"

"I had no choice, Father," Brother Tobias said, rolling his eyes toward Beckett and Mendoza.

"You sent them away?" Father Dominick asked Beckett.

"We ain't exactly in the mood for visitors right now," Beckett answered.

"I see," Father Dominick said. "Still, to turn someone away is unthinkable. It is a show of Christian kindness to offer water, food, and shelter to those who ask it of us."

"You're showin' your Christian kindness by takin' care of us," Beckett said. "Now, what about that food? How long does it take your cook to fix a little supper?"

"Forgive me for not mentioning it the moment you came

in," Father Dominick said. "The cook has informed me that your supper is ready."

"Well, now, that's more like it! Why didn't you say somethin'?" Beckett growled. "Come on, Mendoza, let's get somethin' to eat."

"What is this?" Beckett asked, a moment later, when a bowl of beans and a plate of tortillas was set on the table before them.

"This is your supper."

"Is this it? Is this the Christian kindness you was talkin' about? You didn't even offer us no meat?" Beckett growled.

Father Dominick shook his head. "I'm sorry, in this order we do not eat meat. This is our regular fare. We cannot offer you what we do not have."

"I think maybe it is not so bad, Charley," Mendoza said, rolling up a tortilla in his fingers and filling it with the spicy beans.

"Yeah, well, you're a damn pepper-belly yourself so you like that shit," Beckett growled. "Me, now, I'm more of a meat and potatoes man."

Despite Beckett's protest, Mendoza showed no hesitation in eating.

Win and Joe waited about half an hour before they returned to the monastery. Leaving their horses hobbled, they slipped up to one of the side walls.

"What do we do now?" Joe asked.

"Now we climb over the wall," Win replied. Using chinks and holes in the stone facade to provide foot and handholds, Win started up the side of the wall.

"Damn, I was afraid that was what you were going to say," Joe said. He started up behind his brother, the task somewhat more laborious for him, because of his weight and size.

A moment later, both slipped over the top, then dropped to the ground on the inside.

Most of the buildings inside the monastery grounds were dark. Candles and oil for lamps were precious commodities to be used sparingly, though here and there a flickering light did manage to escape. It wasn't totally dark, however, for the moon was full and bright, and the chapel, dormitory, stable, storage, and grain buildings all gleamed in a soft, silver light, like white blooms sprouting from desert cactus.

"You go that way, I'll go this way," Win whispered. Joe nodded, and the two started on their mission.

The night was alive with the long, high-pitched trills and low violalike thrums of the frogs. For counter melodies there were crickets and the long, mournful howl of coyotes. From the stable, a mule brayed and a horse whickered.

With his gun in hand, and staying in the shadows alongside the wall, Win moved toward the chapel. He found a window and looked inside. There, he saw two men with Father Dominick. The men were pointing their pistols at Father Dominick, who was holding a jewel-encrusted, silver chalice and gold cross clutched tightly to his chest.

"Please, Señor Beckett," he heard Father Dominick's pleading voice. "You can not take the chalice and the cross. They are sacred relics, given to the service of God by the King of Spain more than two hundred years ago. Ten Abbots before me have kept them safe. I will not be the one who loses them."

"They're worth some money, ain't they?" Beckett asked.

"Yes."

"Then we're takin' 'em."

"You will have to kill me first," Father Dominick insisted.

Mendoza laughed, a high-pitched, rather insane chuckle. "You hear that, Charley? We'll have to kill him."

"Well hell, preacher man, that ain't goin' to be no problem," Beckett said. "Julio likes to kill, don't you, Julio?"

"Si, Señor," Mendoza said. He cocked his pistol, then pointed it at Father Dominick.

"Hold it!" Win shouted. Win was still outside the chapel, looking through the window, certainly not in the position he wanted to be to challenge them, but he had no choice. They were about to kill Father Dominick.

"What the hell! Who is that?" Mendoza shouted, swinging his gun toward the window. Beckett was standing by the only light in the room, a flickering candle. With danger imminent, he snuffed it out. The inside of the chapel was immediately plunged into darkness.

Win couldn't see anyone inside, but because he was outside, and lighted by the brightness of the moon, he was visible to both Beckett and Mendoza. They fired.

Win felt a hammer-blow to his shoulder. He returned fire, using the flame pattern from inside as his target. He heard someone groan, then fall. A moment later he heard a crash of glass from the other side of the building and he realized that someone had jumped through the window. He hurried around to try and head him off but, to his surprise, suddenly found himself growing very dizzy. After that, everything went black.

Joe was on the far corner of the grounds, sneaking up on the stable, when he heard the gunshots from the chapel. With his own gun in hand, he started running back through the dark, toward the sound of the shooting. He heard a crash of glass, then he saw someone running through the shadows. He also saw Win in a splash of moonlight, and he saw him stagger, then fall.

"Win!" Joe shouted, starting toward his brother. He let the fleeing man run. For the moment, nothing was more important to him than the well-being of his brother.

Charley Beckett was the one who had leaped through the window and escaped into the night. Julio Mendoza was the man Win shot in the exchange of gunfire. Mendoza died before morning, and even though he was an outlaw who had bullied the Brothers of the Monastery and was in the process of stealing their most precious artifacts, the monks prayed over his body and buried him, if not in the consecrated graveyard, at least just outside the wall.

The bullet was taken from Win's shoulder, and he was patched up and tended by the Brothers of the order. Despite their nursing skills, however, Win contracted a fever and began drifting in and out of consciousness. For several hours, Joe didn't know if Win was going to pull through or not, and though he didn't participate in any of the formal prayers for recovery said by the Brothers, he did offer a few simple prayers of his own.

Unable to wait around and do nothing, Joe found things that would keep him busy. Early in the morning of the third day, he was repairing a door on the granary, when he saw Father Dominick coming toward him. He studied the priest's face, trying to determine if the news he bore was good or bad, but Father Dominick was so skilled in the art of stoicism, that it was impossible to tell.

"Brother Joseph," Father Dominick said. Nothing in the tone of his voice imparted any information.

"How is Win?" Joe asked, getting right to the point.

"God has smiled upon us," Father Dominick said. "Your brother will make a full recovery."

Joe smiled. "Thank you," he said.

"No, Brother Joseph. Thank God."

"Yeah," Joe said. "Yeah, I'm goin' to do that. Not the way you fellas do . . . but I promise you, I'm going to do that."

Over the next few days, while waiting for his brother to recover, Joe found much to admire in the way the monks lived their lives. Joe, who always had been much more a man of the soil than Win, particularly enjoyed working in the garden with them. And as he did so, he couldn't help but contrast his own life of danger and violence with the lives of quiet service and selfless devotion lived by the Brothers. He shared his thoughts with Father Dominick.

"The thing is, Father, I haven't always been a good

man," Joe admitted. "I've drunk a lot, whored a lot, and I've killed. Though, mostly, I've only killed those who needed killing."

"It is not for us to judge who needs killing," Father Dominick said. "All are God's children. Do you think He loves some more and others less?"

"I don't know how God could possibly love some of the sons of bitches I've had to kill," Joe said.

"We can never understand the depth of God's love," Dominick said.

Chapter 5

TWO WEEKS LATER

THE TERRIBLE PAIN STOPPED AND A WARMING NUMBNESS set in. It was the numbness that allowed Ray Mosley to keep up with the others on their mad ride away from the holdup. But with the numbness came also a weakness from loss of blood, and by the time they rode into the little town of Braggadocio just before dawn the next morning, Mosley was staying in his saddle only by supreme will.

"Hey, Charley, Ray's about to keel over here," Billy Hooper said. Hooper had taken it on himself to ride beside Mosley, and for the last three hours had held the reins to Mosley's horse, while Mosley used both hands on the pommel just to stay up.

"Stay with him," Charley ordered. Kansas Charley Beckett, never one to stay down long, had recovered from the loss of his partner Julio Mendoza by putting together a gang of outlaws and misfits. With them, he had hit the bank in Commerce, New Mexico.

It had been a very botched bank robbery. One of the tellers tried to run and they shot him, killing him, and a bank customer in the process. With the entire town alerted, there was nothing left to do but scoop up a handful of

money from the open till. That netted them a grand total
of two hundred and six dollars.

The alerted town reacted quickly, and even as they were
mounting their horses, the good citizens of Commerce began shooting at them. Ray Mosley was hit as he climbed
onto his horse, shot by a woman who was firing a rifle
from just inside the door of the hardware store across the
street.

"Maybe we can find a doctor in town to fix him up,"
Jimmy Purcell suggested.

"We don't have time," Charley growled. "That posse's
goin' to be on us like stink on shit if we wait around here."

"He can't go on much longer, Charley. He needs a doctor," Hooper insisted.

"He's gutshot ain't he? He's goin' to die anyway, ain't
he? Takin' him to a doctor just to have him tell us Mosley
is goin' to croak is just goin' to slow us down more."

"You're all heart, Charley," Mosley grunted.

"Yeah, well, we could just drop you off by the side of
the road," Charley explained.

"That's a good idea. Why don't we do that?" Kelly
Sims asked.

"But look, we got to eat, ain't we?" Hooper asked.
"Maybe we could have the doc's woman fix us some hot
grub while he's lookin' at Ray."

"We could do that, couldn't we, Charley. Billy's right.
We got to eat," Purcell said.

"All right, all right," Charley agreed. "We'll stop, but
just for long enough to get somethin' to eat."

It was still pre-dawn dark, but as the five men rode
through the street, their way was lighted by squares of
golden light on the ground, cast through the windows of
the houses where early risers were already beginning to set
to breakfast.

Charley halted them when they reached the end of the
street.

"What is it?" Hooper asked.

"You wanted to take him to the doc, didn't you? Well, that's the doc's house down there," Charley said.

"How do you know?"

"I was here once. You know, as I think back on it, the doc's got him a fine-lookin' woman, too. Don't know how an old fool like him got such a young, pretty wife. I seen 'er the first time. I thought she was his daughter."

The house Charley pointed to was a low, single-story building which set nearly half a block away from the others. A wisp of wood smoke rose from the chimney, carrying with it the aroma of frying bacon.

"Before we ride up there, fellas, take a good look around," Charley said. "Make sure nobody is watchin' us."

The saddles squeaked as the riders twisted to look around. Mosley held on, telling himself there was only a short time left, then he could lay down and rest in a nice, soft bed.

"It looks clear," Purcell said.

"Let's go," Charley replied. He clicked to his horse and the five of them moved slowly across the distance. They stopped just in front of the doctor's house.

FRED ZORN, M.D., the sign read by the door. Charley didn't bother to knock, he just pushed it open and barged in. Kelly Sims and Billy Hooper were right behind him, half-carrying, half-supporting Mosley. Jimmy Purcell brought up the rear, looking around with his pistol drawn, making certain no one had seen them.

"What the—? What is this?" the surprised doctor asked, looking up from his breakfast table. His wife was standing at the stove frying bacon, and she looked around in alarm as well.

"Don't get fretted none, doc," Charley said. "I'm Charley Beckett. I reckon you've heard of me."

"Kansas Charley!" Dr. Zorn gasped. "Yes, yes, of course I've heard of you."

Beckett's pictures decorated Wanted posters all over the

Southwest, and as "Kansas Charley," he had been glamorized by being the subject of a half-dozen dime novels.

Charley grinned broadly. "Yeah, Kansas Charley, that's me," he said. He was proud of his notoriety, and, even though he couldn't read, he had a copy of each of the novels that had been written about him. "One of my men got hisself pretty bad shot up yesterday afternoon. He needs some doctorin'." Charley looked over toward the stove. "And the rest of us need some grub."

"What makes you think I would . . ." Dr. Zorn started, then he stopped and sighed. "Never mind, put him on the bed. Let me take a look at him."

Hooper and Sims put Mosley on the bed. Dr. Zorn sat beside him, then opened Mosley's shirt.

"He's lucky," he said. "I don't think there's any festering. But the bullet is going to have to come out."

"Hell, why bother?" Charley asked. "He's gutshot. That means he's goin' to die."

"Not necessarily. If I can get the bullet out and he doesn't start festering, he's got a chance."

"You want to waste your time on him, go right ahead. Me, I want somethin' to eat. Miss?"

"There's bacon and a skillet," the doctor's wife said. "And a basket of fresh eggs. There's also a pan of biscuits, fresh made. If you want breakfast, fix it yourself. I have to help my husband tend to this man's wound."

Charley pulled his pistol and pointed it at Mosley. "Well hell, if that's all that's gettin' in the way of us gettin' a little grub, I can just put him out of his misery now."

Dr. Zorn stepped between Charley and Mosley. "If you shoot him, you're goin' to have to shoot me too," he said.

"All right by me," Charley said easily.

"And me," the woman added, stepping in front of her husband.

Charley looked at them for a moment longer, then chuckled. "All right, have it your way. Billy, you fix the breakfast."

"Why me? I ain't no cook."

"I said fix the goddamn breakfast," Charley said, his voice flat and cold. "You the one wanted to get Ray tended to."

"All right, all right," Hooper mumbled.

"Doc, you not only got yourself a young, pretty woman, you got a brave one, too," Charley said. "How did an old fart like you get someone like that?"

When Dr. Zorn didn't answer, Charley gave them both an insolent smile and nod, then walked over to join the others at the kitchen stove.

"Here's a little laudanum," Dr. Zorn said to Mosley, handing him a small bottle. "Take it. You'll need it when I start probing for the bullet."

With his wife assisting, Dr. Zorn removed Mosley's shirt, then began digging in the wound for the bullet. Charley, Hooper, Purcell, and Sims ate their breakfast, totally unconcerned with what was happening over on the bed. A few minutes later Zorn announced that he had the bullet and dropped it with a clink into the pan of warm water. The bullet lay in the bottom of the pan with tiny bubbles of blood rising to paint a swirl of red on the water's surface. No one at the breakfast table seemed particularly interested in the medical report.

"You 'bout finished over there, Doc?" Charley asked, coming from the table, carrying a sandwich made from bacon and a biscuit.

"I've got the bullet out."

"Good, get him patched up so we can put him back on his horse."

"This man can't go anywhere," Dr. Zorn said. "Why, if you take him out of here now, it'll kill him."

"He knew the chances, just like the rest of us," Charley said. "Ray," Charley said gruffly. "Come on, Ray. Get up!"

Mosley groaned.

"Why don't we leave him here, like the doc said?" Hooper asked.

"We can't do that. He knows where we're goin'. He might talk."

"Mosley won't talk," Hooper said. "He's a good man, he won't talk."

"We killed two people in that holdup," Charley said. "That means if we get caught, we're goin' to hang. If they tell him they won't hang him if he'll help 'em find us, are you tellin' me he won't talk?"

"Well, what are we goin' to do?" Hooper asked. "If we can't take him with us and we can't leave him here?"

Charley looked at Mosley, who was now unconscious. Then, without a word, and with as little thought as if he were stepping on a roach, he picked up a pillow and pushed it down over Mosley's face.

"What? What are you doing?" the doctor's wife gasped in shock. She reached for Charley, but he hit her in the face with a wicked backhand, which sent her careening backward, where she bounced off the wall, then slid down into a sitting position.

"Stop!" Dr. Zorn said. "Stop, you're going to kill him!"

"Yeah, Doc, that's what I aim to do," Charley answered with a giggle.

Mosley began to struggle beneath the pillow and Charley pressed it down harder.

"Charley, look out!" Sims suddenly called, and Charley looked over to see Dr. Zorn fumbling desperately with a shotgun, trying to close the breech.

Charley pulled his pistol and fired, his bullet hitting Zorn right between the eyes. The doctor's wife screamed and Charley turned toward her.

"Shut up!" he shouted. "Shut up!"

She screamed again.

Charley fired a second time and the woman quit screaming. A tiny black hole appeared just over her left breast. A trickle of blood oozed down from the hole and her head slumped back against the wall, her eyes open and sightless.

"Shit!" Charley said. "I didn't want to do that. I'd planned to have a little fun with her first."

Outside and all through the neighborhood, dogs began to bark.

"What was that?" a distant voice called.

"Charley, we better get outta here!" Purcell warned. "The whole town's done been woke up."

"What about Ray?" Hooper asked.

Beckett took the pillow away from Mosley's face, then shot him between the eyes.

"What about him?" Beckett asked coldly.

Outside, they could hear dogs barking and people shouting.

"I think those shots come from the doc's house," they heard someone call.

"Let's get out of here," Beckett said.

At Charley's command, the four outlaws bolted through the front door, then vaulted up onto their horses. With the sun showing streaks of red in the eastern sky, they galloped out of town past a dozen or more townspeople, who were by then hurrying down to the doctor's house to see the carnage that had been left behind.

THREE NIGHTS LATER

"You check the horses?" Purcell asked as Hooper came walking back into camp. "They could'a got loose in that storm last night. I wouldn't want to be out here on foot."

"They didn't go nowhere," Hooper said. He sat down on a rock and picked up a stick to begin poking in the dirt. "Where do you think Charley is? You think he's somewhere spendin' our money? I wouldn't put it past the son of a bitch."

"You want to accuse him of that when he gets back?" Purcell asked.

"*If* he gets back," Hooper said with a growl.

"He'll be back," Purcell said. "He's just out checkin' to see if anyone's on our trail. I figure that storm last night done us more good than about anythin'. It for sure wiped out our tracks so's no one could trail us. A week or two with no trail to speak of and things are sure to calm down."

"How the hell you expect anything to die down? We killed two people in the bank holdup, then the doctor and his wife, to say nothin' of Ray Mosley."

Purcell chuckled. "Hell, you don't think anyone got upset 'bout us killin' Mosley, do you?"

"Maybe not . . . but we done enough other stuff to have the whole world lookin' for us," Hooper suggested.

"Yeah, well, if you hadn't insisted we get Ray a doctor, we wouldn't'a had to kill the doctor and his wife," Purcell accused.

"Mosley was hurtin' somethin' awful," Hooper said. "You wouldn't let a horse suffer like he was."

"You'd shoot a horse," Sims suggested.

"Yeah, well Charley offered to shoot the son of a bitch," Purcell suggested. "But you wouldn't have none of it. Now, look where we are, scurryin' around out here like hunted animals, with practically no money a'tall." He leaned over the fire and looked at the meat he was roasting. "This here rabbit looks about done."

"This is a hell of a breakfast, ain't it? I'm gettin' damned tired of rabbit and squirrel and prairie chicken and the like," Hooper growled. "I want a steak."

"And people in hell want ice water," Sims said. "Shut up your bitchin'. You don't want any rabbit, fine. Me an' Purcell will eat your part."

"Didn't say I wasn't goin' to eat it. Just said I was tired of it."

Hooper took out his knife and started to cut off a piece of rabbit. Just as he did so, however, there was a loud popping sound, then the smack of a bullet crashing into the rabbit. Pieces of the rabbit flew in every direction.

Hooper let out a shout of fear and alarm and jumped back from the rabbit. The other two men jumped up and pulled their guns.

"Just drop 'em right there," a voice called.

"What the hell? Who are you, mister? Show yourself!" Sims shouted.

There was another gunshot, and this time the bullet hit the ground right between Sim's feet, then ricocheted up between his legs and whined out over the open prairie.

"I'll take off your balls with the next shot," the voice growled.

"No, no!" Sims said, dropping his gun and raising his hands. "We give up! We give up!"

Purcell and Hooper dropped their guns and raised their hands as well.

"That's more like it," the disembodied voice said. There was the sound of boots walking on rocky ground, then two men appeared from behind a rock. One of them was carrying handcuffs, and he tossed them forward. "How about you fellas trying these on for size?" he asked. He looked around the camp. "Where's Beckett?"

"The son of a bitch skedaddled on us," Hooper said. "With our money." Hooper squinted as he stared at the two men. "Who the hell are you? You aren't the law."

"I reckon not. I'm Win Coulter. This here is my brother, Joe. You boys stirred up quite a ruckus when you robbed that bank in Commerce. You're worth five-hundred dollars apiece."

"Win and Joe Coulter? You the ones they call the Bushwhackers, ain't you?" Sims asked.

"We've been called that," Win agreed.

"Since when did you boys become bounty hunters? Way I've heard it, you walk on the wrong side of the law more often than not."

"Bounty hunting isn't something we're goin' to do, per-

manent,'' Win said. ''Just long enough to see Charley
Beckett dead.''

''Well, hell, what's that got to do with us? You can see,
he ain't here.''

''Maybe not, but you boys had the bad luck to be with
him,'' Win said. ''We were looking for him and we just
naturally found you. And, like I said, you're worth five-
hundred dollars apiece. When we see money like that, we
have to pick it up. Get 'em mounted, Joe.''

Joe took his rope and made three nooses. He put the
nooses around the necks of each of his prisoners, before
ordering them to mount up. As Hooper started to get on
his horse, he slipped, causing a pull against the neck of the
other two men.

''Careful there, you dumb bastard!'' Purcell growled.
''You want to break all our necks?''

Once all three prisoners were mounted, Joe tied the end
of the rope to his saddle, then he swung up onto his horse.

''Okay, gents,'' he said easily. ''Let's head for Commerce. And I would suggest that you all stay together. If
one of you tries to run . . . you're just likely to break the
necks of all three.''

Chapter 6

WIN COULTER WATCHED THE DUST RISE FROM THE HOOF falls of his three prisoners, and he thought about the fact that Charley Beckett was still a free man. Purcell had taunted them about it, obviously trying to get a rise out of Win or Joe. What Purcell didn't realize was that he came much closer than he expected, because the subject of Charles Beckett was even more sensitive now than it had been when he and Joe had started their quests.

There was seldom a day that went by that he didn't think about Beckett, and whenever he rode into a new town, he found that he was always looking for a big man with yellow eyes, a drooping eyelid, and a puffed, ugly scar.

Win looked over at his brother, and wondered if Joe was as tired as he was. It wasn't just the ass-sore tiredness of a long, hard ride. It was the kind of bone-deep weariness that comes on a man after years of riding the trail with one dusty town behind his back and another just ahead. The bad side of it was that it would never get any better. The good side was that, at this stage, it could get no worse.

This anchorless drifting had become a part of the Coulter brothers' heritage. They were men redefined by the saloons, cow towns, stables, manure-piled streets, and open prairies they had encountered. They could not deny this without denying their own existence, and, in fact, had no intention of ever doing so. They were a long way from home, both in time and distance, and yet they were as close to home as the nearest hotel, back room of a saloon, or whore's bed.

"Hey, Coulter, you two goin' to push us all night, or are we goin' to get a chance to rest a bit?" Purcell asked.

"Just keep movin'," Win growled. "We'll be there by midnight."

"Midnight?" Purcell complained. "What the hell? You jumped us 'fore daylight this mornin'. You got no right to push us 'till midnight. I've heard tell that peace officers have to give their prisoners proper rest, food, an' water."

Joe laughed. "Well there you go, mister. Neither one of us are peace officers," he said. "Besides, I wouldn't be worryin' a whole lot about rest if I was you. You and your friends will be getting an eternity of rest in just about a week or so."

"Yeah? Well, we'll see about that," Purcell replied.

"Purcell, you said if we teemed up with Charley Beckett they'd never catch us." Sims whimpered. "I don't want to hang, Purcell. You hear me? I don't want to hang."

"Shut up, Kelly," Purcell said. "Ain't nothin' to be gained by whimperin'."

"All of you keep quiet," Joe said. "I'm not in any mood to listen to your prattle."

"How 'bout if I sing a little song?" Hooper started. "Buffalo Gals won't you come out tonight, come out tonight, come out—uhnn!"

The sudden end to his song was brought on by Joe jerking hard on the rope. As the rope was looped around Hooper's neck, it had the effect of choking off his efforts.

"Watch it!" Hooper said. "If you ain't careful, you could jerk me off here an' break my neck!"

"Really? Well, now, I wouldn't want to do that now, would I, Billy?" Joe said. "That would spoil everyone's fun in watching you hang."

"I hate disappointin' all those nice folks like that, Coulter,'' Purcell said with a growl. ''But I ain't plannin' on givin' them a show.''

Despite the protests, Win and Joe pushed their three prisoners far into the night, arriving in Commerce so late that three of the four saloons were already dark, and the fourth, though still showing light from the bottom floor, was quiet. The horses plodded down the dirt street, the hollow clopping echoing back from the darkened false-fronted stores and houses. From the back of one of the houses a baby cried, and Win heard the cooing sound of its mother going to comfort it. Such sounds barely penetrated Win's cognizance. He was aware that another world existed outside the world he and his brother occupied. He knew there was an entire world of husbands and wives, children and homes, schools, churches, and socials, but such things were so remote from his own experience that he was unable to even dredge up a twinge of envy or regret for his exclusion.

The jail, like the other buildings in town, was dark. They stopped in front, and Win swung down from his horse.

''Ha!'' Purcell barked in what might have been a laugh. ''The sheriff an' his deputies have all gone home for the night. You're goin' to have to bring us back tomorrow.''

''You could take us over to the hotel, maybe rent us a room,'' Hooper suggested.

''Hotel, hell! How 'bout takin' us down to the saloon? We could prob'ly find some whores that's share their bed with us tonight,'' Purcell said.

''Don't know 'bout these two boys, though,'' Hooper added. ''What self-respectin' whore would have anythin' to do with either one of them?''

Win tied his horse off at the hitch rail, then stepped up onto the wooden porch in front of the jail. His boots clumped loudly across the boards. When his horse whiskered, he spun around quickly, his pistol in hand, the hammer pulled back. Just as he had suspected, the three were trying to ease out of the hitch. Joe gave a jerk and all three of them felt it in their necks.

"Hold it, hold it!" Purcell said. "We ain't planning on goin' nowhere!"

"Purcell, that's just about the first true words you've spoken," Joe said. "You ain't goin' nowhere." He emphasized his comment with another jerk on the rope, hard enough to make all three men grunt in protest.

Seeing that his brother had things well in control, Win turned around and banged loudly on the front door of the jail house.

"What do you want?" a muffled voice called from inside.

"Open the door. I've got some prisoners for you."

"Prisoners? We wasn't expectin' no prisoners. Who might they be?"

"Jimmy Purcell, Kelly Sims, Billy Hooper," Sam answered.

"What the hell? You got them?" the voice called. Win could hear footsteps from inside. A key rattled in the lock, and a moment later the door opened. A man, obviously rousted from sleep, stood there, wearing boots and a pair of long underwear. "Who are you?" he asked.

"I'm Win Coulter." Win nodded toward Joe. "The handsome fella hanging onto the rope is my brother, Joe."

"Coulter? Wait a minute. Are you two boys the ones they call the Bushwhackers?"

"You going to take these prisoners or not?"

"Yes, yes sir, I'll take them," the man said. "I'm Deputy Dave Slocum, Mr. Coulter. Boy, oh boy, is Sheriff McQuade goin' to be surprised, come mornin'."

The deputy reached up beside the door. When he pulled his hand back, it was clutched around a Greener ten-gauge shotgun. He pointed the double-barrelled weapon at the three men.

"Okay, you boys, just climb on down real easy now," he said. "I've got a nice room all ready for you."

"These men are worth five-hundred dollars each," Win said. "I'll be needing you to sign a receipt."

"I ain't got no money to give you two boys, Mr. Coulter. I'm just the deputy 'round here."

"That's all right," Win said. "All you have to do is sign the receipt, tellin' that we brought them in. We'll take care of the rest."

"Sure thing. I'll be proud to do that soon as I get these critters locked up. Come along, boys." He jabbed one of them with a shotgun

"Hey, watch it. That hurts," Purcell complained.

"Does it?" the deputy asked, jabbing him again. "Well, now, that's too bad."

Fifteen minutes later Win and Joe were standing at the bar over in the Stardust Saloon.

"Got any Old Overholt?" Win asked when the bartender moved down to stand in front of him.

The bartender, who was sucking on a toothpick, nodded without speaking, then turned to pull a bottle down from the wall behind him. He poured a glass and slid it down the bar in front of Win.

"You the fellas that brung in them three killers and robbers a while ago?" the bartender asked.

Win nodded, then tossed the drink down.

"Seen you comin' in," the bartender said. "Me 'n Lily 'n Clara was the onliest ones down here, an' we heard the horses, so we looked out to see who it was."

"Who was they?" one of the two women asked. The lantern light was kind to both of them from where Win stood. Their skin glowed soft and golden, and the dissipation of the life they led didn't show so badly. They both managed to look almost as young as their years.

"Jimmy Purcell, Kelly Sims, and Billy Hooper," Win answered.

"Beckett wasn't with them?" the bartender asked.

"No."

"That's a shame. He's the worst of the bunch. I'd really like to see him brought in."

"We'll get him," Joe said.

"Lots of folks have said that," the bartender replied. "He ain't been got yet."

"We'll get him," Joe said again.

"Well, if you ask me, I'm glad you got some of them," Lily said. She walked down to stand beside Win, and Carla, taking her tip from Lily, walked down to stand next to Joe. "Karl, pour these two fellas another drink, on us," Lily said.

"Thanks," Win replied, as Karl refilled the glasses.

"It was bad enough them killin' that teller and poor Mr. Hancock when they robbed the bank here," Carla said. "But I heard what they done over in Braggadocio to that poor Dr. Zorn and his wife. And the Zorns doin' no more than their Christian duty to succor the wounded. Whenever Beckett finally is caught, his will be one hanging that I don't aim to miss."

The light was less kind to the two women up close, but there was still something appealing about them. Maybe it was the good humor in their eyes, still alive despite the brutality of their profession. Maybe it was the swell of breasts, soft and inviting to someone many weeks on the trail. Or maybe the two boys were just bone-tired and needed someone to help them make it through the rest of the night.

There were no preliminaries. When Lily led Joe upstairs to her room, both knew why they were going, and the moment they were inside the door, Lily turned to Joe with an open-mouthed kiss. She pressed her body hard against his and sought out his tongue with her own.

Joe's arms wound around her tightly, and he felt the heat of her body transferring itself to him. His blood ran hot as she ground her pelvis against his erection.

Lily stepped away from him just long enough to peel out

of her clothes. Because she was wearing nothing beneath the dress, she was quickly nude, her body glowing golden in the soft light of the lantern that burned dimly on the bedside table.

Down the hall, in the corner room, Win was just lowering himself over Carla.

"Oh, yes . . . put it in me. I want it, now!" Carla was moaning.

Win felt himself slip into the moist box as her pelvic muscles tightened and relaxed and tightened again. Carla was practiced in the art of making love, and, as he entered her, she squeezed herself down on each inch after swollen inch to produce greater sensation.

"All of it!" she pleaded, putting her hands on his butt to pull him into her. Win pushed himself all the way in, and as he did so, Carla shuddered as she rose to climax. Her climax brought a sudden spurting release from Win, and he felt himself draining as he spent himself inside her.

Win collapsed across her, breathing hard for a few moments before finally rolling to one side. They lay together for a few moments, then Win chuckled.

"What is it?" Carla asked.

"I don't believe we ever asked how much this was going to cost us."

"Fifty dollars," Carla said.

Instantly, Win was on one elbow, looking down at her. "Fifty dollars?" he gasped.

Carla smiled. "Why not? I figure it's too late for you to back out now."

"I can't afford fifty dollars," Win said. His fingers rounded the nipple of her breast, and he began to play with it, causing tingling sensations to move through her body. "I might just have to give it back."

"You can do that?" Carla asked. Her hand found his penis, already growing hard again. "Oh, my!" she said in admiration. "You *can* do it."

Chapter 7

"ALL RISE!"

There was a scrape of chairs, a rustle of pants, petticoats, and skirts as the spectators in the courtroom stood. A spittoon rang as one male member of the gallery made a last-second, accurate expectoration of his tobacco quid.

"Oyez, oyez, oyez. This court is now in session. The Honorable Amon Smiley presiding."

The gallery was limited to fifty spectators, and tickets for attendance were highly prized commodities. Most people agreed that Judge Smiley's performances were the best show anywhere, not because of any particular showmanship, but because of his hard-nosed treatment of criminals. He had sentenced so many hardened criminals to hang that he was known far and wide as "King of the Gallows."

Judge Smiley stepped through a rear door and viewed his court. He wasn't a tall man, but he was robust, with a square face and piercing blue eyes. He moved quickly to the bench, then sat down.

"Be seated," he said.

The gallery sat, then watched with interest as first the prisoners were brought into the room, and then the jury.

The jury, composed of twelve men, good and true, had listened to testimony from witnesses to the bank robbery and from the citizens of Braggadocio. The witnesses from Braggadocio told of hearing shots and seeing Charley Harris, Jimmy Purcell, Billy Hooper, and Kelly Sims ride away from the doctor's house. These same witnesses also testified that they found the doctor and his wife dead, along with a fifth member of their gang, Ray Mosley.

Now the jury was ready to render their verdict.

"Gentlemen of the jury, have you reached a verdict?" Judge Smiley asked.

"We have, Your Honor," the foreman answered.

"Please publish the verdict."

"We find the defendants, Jimmy Purcell, Billy Hooper, and Kelly Sims, guilty of murder in the first degree, Your Honor."

"By God, you won't be hanging me!" Purcell shouted.

"Bailiff, silence that prisoner," Judge Smiley said.

The bailiff glared at Purcell.

"Bailiff, would you position the prisoners before the bench for sentencing, please?" Judge Smiley said.

"Yes, Your Honor."

The three men were brought before the bench, where they stood with their heads bowed, contritely.

The judge picked up his gavel and banged it once.

"I sentence you three men, Kelly Sims, Billy Hooper, and Jimmy Purcell, to be hanged by the neck until you be dead. Sentence will be carried out at two o'clock on this very afternoon."

There was a buzz of whispering excitement throughout the court as everyone realized that on that very day there would be a multiple hanging of three prisoners.

"Three! Three at one time, by God!" someone said excitedly.

"Silence! Silence in the court," Judge Smiley said, and again, he slapped his gavel against the pad. The gallery grew quiet. "Deputy, escort the condemned men to the holding cells. Court is dismissed."

"Who'll have tickets to the hanging?" the clerk called.

"Me! I want one!" someone called.

"Save one for me!"

The three prisoners, their legs hobbled with an eighteen-inch chain were chained together for the move back to the cells. As the deputy escorted them out of the court and to the holding cell, they moved with an awkward gait. They shuffled out as crowds of people pressed around the clerk to get the little blue ticket which would grant them access to the side courtyard where the hanging would take place.

The holding cell was separate from the main jail. It was out in the side courtyard, less than fifty feet from the gallows itself. There, the condemned prisoners would be able to look through the barred windows and watch the crowd gather and the excitement grow as time for their execution approached.

The deputy took them out through the side door of the courthouse, then across the sun-baked, dirt-packed courtyard toward the little holding cell. It was quiet in the yard, since, as yet, no spectators had been allowed around the gallows.

As they passed through the shadow of the gallows, they saw someone up on the gallows deck, oiling the hinges to the trap door. He pulled the lever and the door swung open with a bang. Hooper let out a little cry of alarm. The bailiff laughed.

"Don't you fret none, Billy boy," the deputy teased. "They're just greasin' the doors to hell for you." He laughed out loud at his own joke.

"You're gettin' a big kick out of this, ain't you, Dave?" Purcell said to the deputy.

"Oh, yeah," The deputy answered, smiling broadly. "Watchin' you three boys hang is goin' to be like Christmas, New Years, and my birthday all rolled into one," he said.

"Dave, I sure hope nothin' happens to upset your little plans," Purcell said.

The deputy laughed out loud. "Still makin' the jokes, I

see, eh, Purcell? Well, you may as well enjoy what time you got left. I sure plan to.''

"I'm glad I can be so entertainin'," Purcell said. He pointed toward the outhouse. "Hey Dave, before you put us in our cells, how about lettin' me take a leak?''

"You just wait a while," the deputy answered.

"Accordin' to what the judge just said, I don't have all that long to wait for anything," Purcell replied. "Besides, you want me to pee in my pants? Now, that would be a pretty sight for the ladies that come to see the hangin', won't it?''

The deputy looked around the courtyard. Except for the worker on the gallows, no one else was in sight.

"All right," he finally relented. "I'll let you take a leak. But be quick about it.''

"Thanks," Purcell said. "You are goin' to cut me loose from the others, aren't you? I don't care to have them all goin' in there with me.''

The deputy laughed. "Why, Purcell, I never knew you were such a shy man," he said. He bent down to unlock the chain. He didn't notice that the man who had been working on the gallows had come down and was walking over toward him. As soon as he was even with the deputy, he pulled a gun and pointed it at Dave's head.

"Unlock the hobble-chain too," the gallows worker said. "And get the others.''

The deputy looked up in surprise, then his face reflected his shock.

"Beckett!" he gasped.

"Charley, you come for us!" Hooper said.

"Sure, I come for you. You boys didn't think I was goin' to let my pards hang, did you?''

"I have to admit, I had my doubts," Sims said happily.

"Me, too," Hooper added.

There were four horses tied up behind the courthouse.

"We'd best hurry," Beckett urged. "I had to knife the guard at the back gate.''

Suddenly two guards came into the courtyard from the front of the building.

"Stop!" one of them shouted. He fired a shot, which missed. Beckett returned fire and he didn't miss. The guard who had fired collapsed with a hole in his chest. The other guard, suddenly realizing that he was alone, retreated back around the corner.

"We've got to get out of here!" Hooper shouted.

"Wait a minute," Purcell said. "I got a little business to take care of first." He looked at the deputy and started smiling.

The deputy, realizing what was on Purcell's mind, began to tremble in fear, and he held his hands out in front of him.

"Now, Jimmy, you don't want to shoot me," he said. "What good will that do you?"

"Oh, it'll do me a world of good, Dave. More good than you'll ever know," Purcell said with a broad, evil smile. He raised his gun and fired. A bullet hole appeared in the deputy's forehead, then he pitched back.

"Come on, boys, let's ride!" Beckett shouted, swinging into his saddle.

By now the shouts and gunfire had alerted the others, and several armed men appeared in the courtyard, just in time to see the four riders gallop through the back gate. They fired at the outlaws, but not one bullet found its mark. Kansas Charley Beckett and the entire band had gotten away.

Chapter 8

NEARLY THREE-HUNDRED PEOPLE, WHO HAD NOT YET heard of the mass escape, came to see the three men hanged. When they learned that the condemned prisoners had escaped, they were openly vocal in their disappointment at being cheated out of such a grand spectacle.

There was one condemned prisoner, a man named Bryant, who had raped and murdered a school marm. He wasn't due to die for one more week, but because the gallows had already been built and because Judge Smiley didn't want to disappoint the people, he moved the hanging up. With the others gone, Bryant was the only show in town.

"At least we're goin' to see a hanging of some kind," the citizens told each other. "I mean, it ain't like comin' into town was a total waste."

On the second floor of the courtroom, Judge Smiley stood at the window of his chambers, looking down on the milling crowd. Win and Joe were just behind him. Joe lit a cigar, which he had just extracted from a humidor on the Judge's desk.

"I told you I'd pay the money and I will," Judge Smiley

said without turning around. "There's fifteen hundred dollars in that brown envelope on my desk."

Win reached for it.

"The territory will pay another fifteen hundred to get them back, and I'll see to it that the court adds fifteen hundred more. That's a total of forty-five hundred dollars," Smiley said.

"Forty-five hundred dollars?" Win said. "You know, Judge, with that kind of reward money out there, you're just going to make it harder to find them. There will be too many people who don't know what they are doing, trying to get the reward. They'll just be getting in the way."

Judge Smiley turned away from the window. "That reward isn't for everyone," he said. "I'm only offering that to you."

"You're not putting out new dodgers?"

Judge Smiley shook his head. "No," he said.

"Why not? That kind of money is pretty persuasive," Joe replied.

"Like you say, it would just bring in too many amateurs. I particularly want these men," Judge Smiley said. "The reward is for dead or alive," Judge Smiley said. "But if you can, I want them alive. I want to hang these men."

"Where Beckett is concerned, we make no promises," Win said.

"You'll at least try to get them here alive?"

"Like I said, where Beckett is concerned, we make no promises," Win said again.

Judge Smiley stroked his chin for a long moment before he answered.

"All right," he said. "I've sentenced them to die, I guess the manner of their execution doesn't really matter. You do whatever it takes."

Johnny Bryant looked around defiantly as he was led to the gallows. He was wearing a gray, collarless shirt and gray trousers. His legs weren't hobbled, but his hands were cuffed behind his back. He squirted out a stream of tobacco juice just as he reached the foot of the thirteen steps, then he hesitated.

"This ain't fair," Bryant said. "I wasn't supposed to hang 'til next week."

"Get on up there, Bryant," Sheriff McQuade said. "You done your killin' like a man, now die like one."

Bryant turned around to glare at him. "Sheriff, you don't have to give me no lessons on how to die," he said.

"Come on, Johnny," McQuade said more gently. "The sooner we get this over with, the better it is for all of us."

Bryant moved onto the scaffold, then was positioned under the noose. The scaffold had been built for a multiple hanging, and it looked somewhat unbalanced with him standing at one end. From here, Bryant had a very good look into the faces of the spectators, and he glared at them defiantly.

The clergyman who was on hand for the hanging walked up to Bryant.

"Mr. Bryant, do you want to repent?" the clergyman asked.

"What have I got to repent for?"

"Why, you have killed, sir."

Bryant looked out over the faces of the crowd. "Yeah? Well, what do you think they are about to do to me?"

"The authorities are merely executing their God-given right," the preacher said.

"And the folks here? Is it their God-given right to enjoy watchin' me dance?"

"I beg of you, Sir. Repent. Repent now, before it is too late."

"I ain't repentin' for a goddamned thing."

"Mr. Bryant!" the preacher said angrily. "You are goin' to meet God with heresy in your heart and blasphemy on your lips! You'll spend an eternity in hell for that!"

"Thank's for the words, preacher," Bryant said sarcastically. "They're real comfortin'."

The preacher, red-faced with anger, turned and walked quickly off the scaffold.

"Any last words, Bryant?" the sheriff asked. The sheriff was having to serve as the hangman, since Beckett had killed the man who was supposed to do the job.

"Yeah. I wonder what they'll be servin' for supper in hell?" Bryant asked. "Whatever it is, it's bound to be better'n that pig swill you serve in this jail."

"I don't know, but when you get there, say hello to a few of my friends for me, will you?" the sheriff asked.

"Sheriff, you want me to hold you a place at the supper table?" Bryant asked as the black hood was slipped over his head.

The sheriff chuckled. "That's nice of you, Johnny. Real nice," he said. "It's time." He fit the noose. "When the trap opens, don't hunch up your shoulders," he added, trying to be helpful. "Just relax and it'll be better."

"Really? How the hell do you know?" Bryant mumbled from under his hood.

When the sheriff had him ready, he stepped over to the handle that would open the trap door. He glanced up toward the window where Judge Smiley stood looking down. Smiley nodded his head and the hangman pulled the handle.

The trap door swung down on its hinges and Bryant's body dropped about five feet. There was an almost orgasmic gasp from the crowd as the body fell.

Bryant didn't die right away. He was still alive, and for almost four minutes he kept drawing his body up as if in that way he could relieve the weight on his neck. His stomach heaved, and those nearest the scaffold could hear rasping sounds from his throat. Finally his body was still.

"Ghastly business this," Judge Smiley said, pouring himself a drink with shaking hands. He looked over at Win and Joe. "You two men live your life right on the edge, don't you?"

"You might say that," Win agreed.

Judge Smiley tossed his drink down. "Watch your step,"

he said. "I wouldn't want to ever see either one or both of you up there on my gallows."

"Don't worry, Judge," Win replied matter-of-factly. "If it ever came to that . . . you wouldn't live long enough to see it."

Nervously, Judge Smiley poured himself another drink.

The sound of a shot rolled down the mountainside, picked up resonance, then echoed back from the neighboring mountains. Charley Beckett, who was holding a smoking pistol, turned toward his audience of three with a smile on his face. He had just broken a discarded whiskey bottle with his marksmanship.

"I'd like to see either one of the Coulter boys do that," he snarled.

"Charley, there ain't nobody said you ain't good with a gun," Hooper said. "Maybe even as good as the Coulters, but . . ."

"*Maybe* as good? Maybe as good?"

"Well, as good then. Maybe even better—"

"There ain't no maybe to it. I *am* better."

"But even if you are, that don't matter. You shoulda seen how them sneaky bastards come up on us the last time. They got the drop on us afore we even had a notion anyone was anywhere around. I say we don't take no chances this time."

"And what do you propose that we do?" Charley asked.

"I think we ought to split up . . . ever' man for hisself. Them sonsofbitches can't follow us all at the same time."

"No, but they can follow just one of us," Sims pointed out. "And woe betide the one that they follow."

"Yeah? Well, I ain' afraid of either one of the bastards," Beckett said.

"You mean you don't care if they get on your tail?" Hooper asked.

"Hell, when you get right down to it, they been on my tail ever' since the end of the war," Beckett replied. "What

I ought to do is quit runnin'. I ought to just wait behind a rock and shoot them down.''

"You mean you'd shoot them from ambush?'' Hooper asked.

"Hell yes! I don't need to kill the sons of a bitches fair and square . . . I just want to kill them.''

"Charley has a point, Sims said. "The best way to handle the Coulters would be to set up an ambush.''

"No,'' Hooper replied. "I still think it would be best if he didn't even find us at all, and if we split up, we'll have a better chance.''

"Except for the one he comes after,'' Sims pointed out.

"All right,'' Purcell said. "How about this? Instead of all of us separatin', we'll break into two groups. That way he'll still have to make a choice, but even when he does, we won't have to face him alone.''

"All right, I'll go along with that,'' Sims said.

"This is the way we'll do it,'' Charley explained. "Kelly, you and Billy cut out one way, me an' Purcell will go another. Now, whichever ones of us gets wind that he ain't on our trail, why, we'll double back and help out the others. That way, we'll have him pinched right in the middle.''

"Why that's a wonderful idea!'' Hooper said, smiling broadly. He chuckled. "Charley, you should'a been a general.''

Chapter 9

IT WAS FOUR DAYS BEFORE WIN AND JOE CAME ACROSS A fresh trail. The men they were after had split up, two going in one direction, two going in the other. Win and Joe decided not to split up, but to follow one set of tracks.

"They'll probably rejoin somewhere," Win said. "And if they don't, why we'll take care of these two, then go after the others."

"Yeah," Joe agreed. "I just hope Beckett is one of the two men we're following."

Beckett wasn't one of the two. They learned that when they talked to a bartender in Posey. He had recognized Billy Hooper when he stopped for a drink.

Hooper was with another man . . . the bartender wasn't sure who the other man was, but he was sure it wasn't Kansas Charley Beckett.

It was too late now to double back and follow the other trail. They had no choice but to stay on this one and hope that their theory of them eventually rejoining was right.

Hooper and whoever was with him took great pains to cover their true trail, while leaving false trails for the Coulters to follow. They rode through streams and over hard rock, trying every trick in the book to shake off their pursuers but, doggedly, Win and Joe hung on.

Once, while following them through a draw in Red Rock Mesa, Hooper and his partner started a rock slide. It nearly caught Win and Joe, and they had to turn their horses and gallop hard to get out of the way.

"Damn!" Sims said. "We almost got the sons of bitches!"

"Yeah, well, almost ain't good enough," Hooper said. "The bastards are still alive, and they're still after us."

"What are we goin' to do, Billy? You got 'ny ideas?"

"No," Hooper answered.

"What if we just wait behind some rocks somewhere and ambush them?"

Hooper shook his head. "If we don't get them right off, they'll get behind as well, then we'll be in a gunfight with 'em. I don't know about you, Kelly, but I ain't planning' on gettin' in no gunfight with the likes of Win and Joe Coulter. Not with it bein' just the two of us."

"Yeah, well it ain't supposed to be just the two of us," Sims reminded him. "Charley said him and Purcell would come a' runnin' if they seen that the Coulters wasn't after them. Remember?"

"Yeah? Well where the hell are they?" Hooper asked. "Do you see any sign of 'em?"

"No," Sims admitted.

"No, an' you ain't likely to," Hooper told him. "Them two sonsofbitches have run out on us."

Twenty Miles South

"Did you see anything back there, Purcell?" Beckett asked when Purcell scrambled back down from the promontory, his boots dislodging pebbles and small rocks.

"No, nothin'," Purcell replied. He brushed his hands together. "I looked as far as I could in all directions, and I didn't see even a piece of a dust plume. I don't think they're followin' us."

Beckett took a drink of water, wiped the back of his hand

across his mouth, then corked his canteen and hooked it back on the saddle pommel.

"Well, then he must've lit out after Hooper and Sims."

"We goin' to double back?" Purcell asked.

"Double back? What for?"

"You said we was goin' to double back if we seen that the Coulters wasn't doggin' us."

"Far's I'm concerned, Hooper and Sims is on their own. Unless you want to go back and tangle with the Coulter boys."

"You think I'm crazy? If you ain't goin' back, I sure as hell ain't."

"I didn't figure you was that dumb," Charley said.

"Anyway, the way I look at it, by the Coulters takin' out after them like they done, just makes it all the better for us."

"Yeah," Purcell said. He smiled. "Yeah, I guess you're right at that. While Hooper and Sims is keeping the Coulters busy, we'll be runnin'. The question is, where will we be runnin' to?"

"You ever heard of the town of Bertrand?"

"No, can't say as I have."

"Well, it's a little flyspeck of a town not too far from here," Beckett said. "There's a man there, name of Marcus Scruggs. He's a good man with a gun, and an old pard of mine. When I left the bunch of you before, I sent Scruggs a wire, askin' him to join up with us. If the Coulters run into us, it might come in handy to have an extra gun."

"We had two extra guns, and you sent 'em off," Purcell said.

"Yeah, but it worked out fine, what with the Coulters goin' after them. Besides, both them together ain't as good a gun as Scruggs."

"What makes you think Scruggs would join us? Who would just volunteer to start runnin' from the Coulters?"

"Scruggs is good with a gun, but he ain't too swift up here," Beckett said, tapping the side of his head. "He needs someone to figure out things for him. I figure we'll join up in Bertrand, then move over to a little town not too far from here, called Dorena. We'll rob the bank there. Then we'll not only have an extra gun ridin' with us . . . we'll have some money to spend.''

"Dorena? Never heard of it. How big is it?''

"No more'n two or three-hundred people.''

"No more'n two or three-hundred? How much money could be in a bank like that?'' Hooper asked.

"Well, how much you got now?'' Beckett asked.

"Not much,'' Purcell admitted.

"So whatever we get ought to sound pretty good, don't you think?'' Beckett asked. "Besides, I'm talkin' about a real cracker box of a bank. Prob'ly ain't nobody ever even thought about robbin' it. Hell, the folks will be so surprised, they'll piss in their pants when they see us.''

TWENTY MILES NORTH

"They're still comin',"" Sims said.

Hooper twisted around in his saddle. "How far back are they? Can you see 'em?''

"Yeah, I got a glimpse of 'em just over the last ridge.''

"That'd make 'em less'n a mile back.''

"Ain't they no way we can shake 'em?'' Sims asked.

"You got 'ny ideas that we ain't tried?'' Hooper replied. "We done ever'thing I can think of, an' it ain't even slowed 'em down none.''

"So what do you want to do now? You want to wait behind a couple of rocks like I suggested?''

"No. I told you, I don't want to get into a gunfight with 'em unless the odds are a little better.''

"Well, pretty soon we ain't goin' to have no choice,'' Sims pointed out. "They're back there, they're comin', and they ain't nothin' on earth goin' to stop 'em from catchin' us. Then we're goin' to have to shoot it out sure enough, only by then they'll be choosing the time and the place.''

"Yeah, well there is one thing we could do," Hooper suggested, "if you're game for it."

"Hell, I'm willin' to try 'bout anythin'," Sims said. "What you got in mind?"

"We could split up again. You go one way and I'll go the other."

"Well now, hold it. That don't make no sense to me at all. I mean here you are, bitchin' 'cause you say two to two ain't the right kind of odds to go up against 'em. But you're wantin' us to split up so it'll be one to one."

"They didn't separate when we split up before. Like as not, they won't split up again. That means curtains for who-ever's trail they dog," Hooper said. "But the other one of us can get away free and clear. That gives each one of us a fifty-fifty chance of not havin' to run into 'em at all. And for whichever one of us that does run into him, well, hell, we won't be that much worse off than we are now."

"Yeah, all right," Sims said, stroking his chin. "I guess them odds is about as good as any. Which way you aimin' to go?"

"I thought I might go west," Hooper said.

"All right, you go west, I'll go south," Sims replied. He smiled crookedly at Hooper. "I ain't goin' to wish you luck," he said. " 'Cause if your luck is runnin' good, that'll mean mine is runnin' bad."

"Yeah," Hooper said. "I know what you mean. Maybe we'll see each other around some time."

"Maybe," Sims replied. He slapped his heels against his horse's flanks, then started down the middle of a small stream, heading south.

Hooper started west, but after a few moments he reined up and looked back to the point where he and Sims had separated. Sims was out of sight now, and, because he had gone down the middle of the stream, there was absolutely no sign that he had been there at all.

Hooper saw a willow tree, its boughs hanging low over the water, and he suddenly got an idea. He rode back into the stream, up to the tree, then he reached up and broke two of the branches. After that he rode back into the rocks, got off his horse and tied it down. He pulled the Winchester from its saddle sheath and bellied down between two rocks, where he not only had cover and concealment, but a good view of the willow tree as well. He jacked a round into the chamber, then piled a couple of rocks on top of each other to make a rest for the rifle. He sighted down the barrel, then waited.

When Win and Joe reached the edge of the stream, they stopped. If the two men they were after followed the pattern they had established, they would use the stream for as long as they could, to avoid leaving a trail. For most trackers that would work. Win and Joe, however, could often follow a trail through the water by paying attention to such things as rocks dislodged against the flow of water or silt, which, when disturbed by horse's hooves would leave a little pattern in the water for several minutes afterward.

Joe was about to check the streambed when he saw something unusual. There were two limbs broken in the willow tree that hung over the bank of the stream.

"Win, look over there," Joe said. He started toward the tree.

"Hold it, little brother," Win called.

Joe stopped. "What is it?"

"Don't you think there's somethin' a little strange about that? In the first place, those limbs should be supple enough not to be broken by someone passing through them. And in the second place, the two men we're tracking haven't done anything as foolish as ride through the brush before now."

"You sayin' the limbs are broke on purpose?" Joe asked.

"Yeah, that's what I'm thinkin'," Win said. At that instant, the hair pricked on the back of his neck. Someone had the drop on them. "Get down!" Win shouted.

Suddenly, and unexpectedly, Win threw himself off his horse. At almost the precise instant he made his move, a rifle boomed and a .44-40 bullet cracked through the air at exactly the place where his head had been but a second earlier.

Win and Joe hit the water feet first, then ran through the stream, splashing silver sheets of spray as they headed for the bank on the opposite side. They zigzagged as they ran and when the rifle boomed a second time, the strike of the bullet in the water demonstrated the wisdom of their erratic motion, for it too hit where, but a second earlier, one of them had been.

The two brothers dived into the tall grass on the bank of the stream, then wriggled toward the protection of a large rock about ten yards away. Though they were concealed by the grass, they weren't protected by it, and a lucky shot would be disastrous.

Win bent over a large cattail, and hooked his hat on top. He found a fairly long branch and used it to hold the cattail down while he backed away from it, moving closer to the protection offered by the boulder. When he was as far away from the cattail as the long branch would let him be, he let go and the cattail, with his hat on top, sprung back to the upright position.

Almost instantly the rifle boomed again and Win saw his hat go flying. Sam used that opportunity to move the last few feet to the boulder. There, he sat with his back against the rock and took a few deep breaths.

"Coulter? Are you hit?"

Win recognized Billy Hooper's voice.

"You weren't even close, Billy," Win called from behind the rock.

Win heard Hooper gasp in surprise, for not only was Win not where Hooper expected him to be, he had also not been hit.

"You son of a bitch!" Hooper shouted. He fired two more times in the vicinity of where he had heard Win's voice, but the bullets whistled harmlessly overhead.

"Why don't you give up, Billy? There's no way you're going to get out of this alive."

"Give up? And go back to be hung?"

Win chuckled. "I'll admit you don't have much to look forward to," he said. "But you may as well know we're taking you out of here, in your saddle or belly-down on it. Now, which is it to be?"

"Let me think about it a moment."

"Don't take too long," Win said.

There was a long moment of silence, then Hooper called again.

"Coulter, you ever thought you 'n your brother might've followed the same trail I rode? Could be you boys was the one with a price on your heads and not me."

"Could've been," Win admitted. "Has been, in fact."

Hooper chuckled. "I just had me an idea that you two boys has run from the law before. I mean, when you stop and think about it, we ain't all that different, are we?"

"Neither one of us ever shot any innocent women," Joe called.

"Yeah, well, if you talkin' about the doc's wife, it was Charley that shot her. None of the rest of us had anything to do with that."

"You didn't make any effort to stop him."

"No, I reckon we didn't," Billy replied.

Suddenly, and unexpectedly, Win heard the sound of horses hooves, and when he raised up and looked around, he saw that Hooper had managed to get mounted and was now galloping toward them. Hooper had his pistol in his hand and he was firing as he rode. One bullet took a nick out of Win's hand, causing him to drop his pistol.

"See you in hell, Coulter!" Hooper shouted, taking dead aim at Win.

From the corner of his eye, Win saw something that Hooper didn't see. Joe had stood up from behind a rock and was pointing his pistol at Hooper.

"Hold it, Billy! I've got the drop on you!" Joe shouted.

Hooper swung his pistol toward Joe and fired. Joe fired back, and Win saw a puff of dust rising from Hooper's vest, followed by a tiny spray of blood. Hooper pitched backward out of his saddle. One foot hung up in the stirrup, and his horse continued to run, raising a plume of water as Hooper was dragged through the stream. As the horse tried to climb the bank out of the water, Hooper's foot disconnected from the stirrup and he lay motionless, half in the water and half out.

Joe ran over to him, his gun still drawn. When he saw that Hooper was unarmed, having lost his pistol during the dragging, Joe holstered his gun and pulled Hooper the rest of the way out of the water. Win came up then, as well, and they were surprised to see that Hooper was still breathing, though the rattle of his breathing told them that the outlaw wouldn't be alive much longer.

"That was a damn fool thing to do," Joe said.

Hooper tried to laugh, but when he did so, bubbles of blood frothed out from the corner of his mouth.

"I reckon it was," he admitted. "But there wasn't no way I was goin' to let you two take me back to be hung. To tell the truth, I was kinda hopin' one of you would shoot me."

"Where are the others?" Win asked.

Hooper, who had closed his eyes in pain, now opened them and looked at Win.

"You think I'm goin' to tell you that?"

"You don't owe any of them anything," Win advised him.

"Hell, Coulter, I know that," Hooper replied. "That ain't the reason I ain't goin' to tell you boys nothin'. I ain't tellin' you nothin' 'cause it's the only way I got now of gettin' at you."

"It makes no difference whether you tell us or not," Win said. "We're goin' to find them. Especially Beckett."

Again Hooper tried to laugh, and again bubbles of blood frothed from his mouth.

"Yeah, you prob'ly will. Fact is, Beckett told me 'bout the little girl him and Mendoza raped and murdered, so I hope you do find the bastard. But if it takes you just one day longer, then I figure I'll have my laugh." Hooper suddenly took two or three gasping breaths, then he died.

Chapter 10

FROM TWO MILES AWAY, WIN AND JOE COULD SEE THE little town of Bertrand baking under the sun. It was hot, dry, dusty, and as brittle as tumbleweed. They had filled their canteens at the stream, and filled Hooper's as well, figuring that since he was belly-down on the horse behind them, he wouldn't mind.

Even with the extra canteen they had rationed their water, but now, with the town in front of them, they let themselves drink the final few swallows. The water was warm, and their tongues were so swollen and dry that any moisture, regardless of temperature, was welcome. And, although they were drinking tepid water, they could almost taste the cool beer they would have in the saloon in town.

Win hooked his canteen back onto the saddle pommel then urged the two horses forward, the one he was riding and the one he was leading. The buildings in the town had collected the day's heat and were now giving it back in waves so that Bertrand seemed to shimmer in the distance. A dust devil developed in front of them, propelled by a wind that felt as if it were blowing straight from the fires of hell. A jackrabbit popped up, ran for several feet, then darted under a dusty clump of mesquite.

"We ever been to this town before, big brother?" Joe asked.

Win shook his head. "Not that I can recall."

"Sure don't seem like much of a town."

"If it's got a saloon, it's town enough," Win said.

Joe chuckled. "You got that right."

It took the better part of a quarter hour to reach the town after they first saw it, and they rode in slowly, sizing it up with wary eyes. It was a town with only one street. The unpainted wood of the few ramshackle buildings was turning gray and splitting. There was no railroad coming into Bertrand, but there was a stagecoach station with a schedule board announcing the arrival and departure of four stage coaches per week. Over the last several years, the two brothers had encountered many towns like this, isolated, inbred, and stagnant.

They rode past the buildings, Win subconsciously enumerating them as he passed. There was a rooming house, a livery, a smithy's, and a general store that said "Drugs, Meats, Goods" on its high, false front. There was a hotel and restaurant, too and, of course, the ubiquitous saloon . . . this one called the Red Star Saloon. Across the street from the saloon was the jail. Win and Joe rode up to the hitching rail in front of the jail. Win dismounted and patted his shirt and pants a few times. The action sent up puffs of white dust, which hovered around him like a cloud. Joe, still mounted, looked up and down the street. A few buildings away a door slammed, while across the street, an isinglass shade came down on the upstairs window of the hotel. A sign creaked in the wind and flies buzzed loudly around the piles of horse manure that lay in the street.

"You stay out here and keep your eyes open," Win said. "I'll see if I can cash Mr. Hooper in."

Joe nodded.

Win pushed open the door. No one was at the desk, but someone was sleeping in a bunk in one of the cells. The door to that cell, like the door to all of them, was standing open. Except for this one, all the cells were empty.

Win walked over to the wall where several posters were tacked and began studying them. He had left the door to the building standing open, and a gust of wind blew it shut with a loud bang.

"What? What?" the man in the cell said, awakened by the sound. He sat up on the bunk and saw Win standing by his poster wall.

"Who are you?" he asked.

Win looked toward him. "You a prisoner?" he asked.

"A prisoner? Hell no I'm not a prisoner," the man said indignantly. "I'm the sheriff, by God!"

"I got a body for you," Win said.

"A body? Where?"

"Belly-down across his horse," Win said. "He's tied up out front."

"Who is it?"

Win saw a poster with Billy Hooper's name and picture, and he tore it down. "This man," he said.

The sheriff, who was bald-headed and overweight, came out of the cell stuffing his shirt down into his trousers. "The hell you say. Billy Hooper, huh? He's a bad one. Did you kill him?"

"My brother did. He's outside with the body."

"I suppose you'll be puttin' in for the reward?"

Win glared at the sheriff. "We didn't kill him for the sport of it," he said.

"No, I don't reckon you did. Well, let me take a look at him and I'll send a wire back," the sheriff said, starting toward the door. "Who will I say is puttin' in for the reward?"

"Coulter. Win and Joe Coulter."

"Coulter?" the sheriff replied. He stared hard at Win. "You the ones they call the Bushwhackers?"

"We're called that, sometimes," Win said. He nodded toward the posters. "Has Charley Beckett been through here?" he asked.

"I wouldn't know if he has or not," the sheriff answered. "But in truth, even if I seen 'im, I would give 'im a wide berth. The only job I got is to keep the peace in Bertrand. I ain't in the man huntin' business. Once I get confirmation to pay you, where will I find you?"

"Soon as we board our horses, we'll be in the saloon just down the street," Win said.

News of the Coulters bringing in Billy Hooper reached the saloon before the two brothers did, so that everyone was talking about them, even before they arrived. Marcus Scruggs overheard the talk as he was eating beans at a table in the back of the saloon. He was planning to leave Bertrand that night, to join up with Charley Beckett, and he thought this might be some information Beckett would want to know.

"Here they come!" someone hissed, and the saloon grew quiet. A moment later, Win and Joe Coulter pushed their way through the bat-wing doors.

Scruggs got an idea. He wasn't sure how good an idea it was . . . there was no one with him he could ask about it. But it was an idea he couldn't shake, and, if he could pull it off, he knew it would go down well with Charley Beckett.

The Coulters didn't know him and wouldn't be expecting anything. Scruggs was good with both a gun and a knife. He was fast, and he was accurate. Everyone told him that. If he just opened up on the two brothers, he was sure he could get them before they got him. In fact, if he used his knife, he might be able to get one of them before the other one even realized he was in danger.

"Give us each a beer," he heard one of them say to the bartender.

The bartender drew the beers and put them on the bar. The bigger of the two brothers, the one Scruggs knew was Joe, blew off the head then drank nearly three-quarters of it before he put it down. Then he wiped his mouth with the back of his hand and turned his back to the bar to look out over the patrons.

Damn! He's looking right at me! Scruggs thought. No, he couldn't be. He was just looking around the room, that's all. There was no way the Coulters could know about him.

Joe looked right toward Scruggs, then passed his eyes around the rest of the room.

If Scruggs was going to get them, he would never have a better chance than now.

Joe finished the beer, then turned toward the barkeep to ask for another when suddenly something flashed by in front of him. It was knife! The blade buried itself about half an inch into the bar with a solid thunk. After that, the handle vibrated back and forth.

Win had also seen the knife coming, and even as the knife was burying itself in the bar, Win had his pistol out and was turning toward the direction from which the knife had come. He saw a man getting up from a table with a gun in his hand. However, when that man saw how quickly Win had drawn, he held his hands up, letting the pistol dangle from its trigger guard.

"No, no," he shouted. "Don't shoot, me, mister. Don't shoot!"

"Why the hell not?" Win growled. "If you would've had your way, my brother would be wearing that Arkansas toothpick by now." Win squinted at Scruggs. "What'd you do that for? We ever run across each other before?"

"No," Scruggs admitted.

"Then why did you try to kill me?" Joe asked.

"Could be I just don't like your looks," Scruggs said.

"That's not much of a reason for killing a man," Joe said.

"I've kilt men for less reason. You have, too, I reckon, from what I've heard of you."

"What have you heard of us?"

"You're the ones they call the Bushwhackers, ain't you?

There's people will pay good money to see you dead."

"Could be," Win admitted. "But you won't be collecting any of it. Drop your gun."

Scruggs made no move to drop his gun.

"Drop it, I said, or I'll kill you where you stand," Win said, menacingly.

Scruggs smiled, then slowly turned the pistol around so that the butt was pointing toward Win.

"You ain't goin' to shoot me," he said. "I've done give up, and this here saloon is full of witnesses who'll swear I was handin' you my gun. You shoot me now, you'll hang."

"Go ahead and shoot the sonofabitch, anyway," Joe said. "We ain't hung yet, and there's been a heap of people try."

Win stared at Scruggs, and for a long moment it looked as if he might actually do it. Then he sighed. "I should do what my brother says. But I'm feeling generous, so I think I'll just take you across the street and throw you in jail until we leave. If you're real nice to the sheriff, he might feed you."

"You ain't scarin' me none, Coulter. I don't mind coolin' my heels here for a while. You goin' to take my gun or ain't you?"

Win started across the floor for Scruggs's gun, but before he had gone half a step, Scruggs executed as neat a border roll as Win had ever seen. Win wasn't often caught by surprise, but this time he was. Not only by the fact that Scruggs would try such a thing, but by the skill with which Scruggs was able to do it.

Joe was standing by the bar without a pistol in his hand, and Win had relaxed his own position to the point where he had actually let the hammer down, and even lowered the gun. Now he had to raise his pistol back into line while at the same time cocking it. And he was slowed by the fact that he first had to react to Scruggs's action.

The quiet room was suddenly shattered with the roar of two pistols snapping firing caps and exploding powder almost simultaneously. The bar patrons yelled and dived or scrambled for cover. White gun smoke billowed out in a cloud that filled the center of the room, momentarily obscuring everything.

As the smoke began to clear, Scruggs stared through the white cloud, smiling broadly at Win. He opened his mouth as if to speak. The only sound he made, however, was a gagging rattle, way back in his throat. The smile left his face, his eyes glazed over, and he pitched forward, his gun clattering to the floor.

Win stood ready to fire a second time if needed, but a second shot wasn't necessary. He looked down at Scruggs for a moment, then holstered his pistol.

There were calls from outside, then the sound of people running. Several came into the saloon and stood under the rising cloud of gunsmoke to stare in wonder at the dead man on the floor. One of the new arrivals was the sheriff.

"Damn me if death don't seem to follow you Coulter boys like a black cloud," the sheriff observed. He pointed at the body on the floor. "I take it, this is your doin'?"

"Yes," Win answered. "I had no choice, you can ask anyone."

"That's right, Sheriff, this here fella shot first," someone said.

The sheriff nodded. "He one of the ones you're after?"

Win shook his head. "Hell, I don't even know who the sonofabitch is."

"His name is Scruggs. Marcus Scruggs," the sheriff said.

"You know him?"

The sheriff nodded. "He's been hanging around town for last two or three months. Pretty much of a bully, but I haven't had any trouble with him before."

"Marcus Scruggs? I don't recognize his name. Is there paper on him, too?"

"I'm not sure," the sheriff replied. "I just sent the wire

about Billy Hooper. I reckon I can send another one askin'
about Scruggs.''

"I'm obliged. I didn't set out to cash him in, but if he's
worth anything, I might as well take it.''

"What about the body?'' the sheriff asked.

Win shrugged. "That's your department now, sheriff.
I'm turning him over to you. Put him alongside Hooper.
They're birds of a feather.'' As Win talked to the sheriff,
he knelt beside Scruggs's body and began going through
the outlaw's pockets.

"I thought you said the body was mine,'' the sheriff said.

"The body is yours,'' Win replied. "What I find in his
pockets is mine. Anyway, you haven't signed the receipt
yet.''

Win found a money clip containing twenty dollars in
paperback currency. In addition to the paper money, there
were fifteen dollars in coin. He handed the coin to the sheriff. "You can use this to bury him,'' he said.

"Thanks,'' the sheriff replied, putting the coins in his
pocket.

Win looked up at the bartender. "You ever know
Scruggs to buy anyone a drink?''

"No,'' the bartender answered. "He was a tight sonofabitch.''

Win gave the twenty dollars in paper to the barkeep.
"Well, he's buyin' drinks now. Set 'em up as long as the
money lasts.''

The bartender smiled broadly. "Yes, sir,'' he said.
"Boys, the drinks are on Scruggs!'' he called.

After Scruggs's body was dragged out of the saloon and
the excitement of the event had died down, Win and Joe
sat at the same table where Scruggs had been sitting and
ordered a meal of bacon, eggs, and coffee.

Back in the kitchen, Joe saw a boy sweeping the floor
and he motioned to him. When the boy came out to the
table, Joe gave him a coin and asked him to take care of

their horses. Their supper had just been put before them when the boy returned.

"I put up your horses, mister," the boy said.

"Thanks."

"Was he a bad man? The one that was killed?"

"Yes," Joe replied.

The boy smiled. "I thought he was. I could tell."

"How could you tell?"

"His eyes," the boy said, moving his fingers across his own eyes. "They were evil. His smile was not happy. He drank a lot and kept watching the door."

"He kept watching the door, you say?" Win asked.

"Yes, sir."

"Thanks. You have a good eye."

The boy smiled proudly. "Someday soon I am going to leave Bertrand and become a great gunfighter, just like you," he said.

"Your mother and dad may want you to wait until you are a little older."

"I have no parents," the boy said.

"Where do you live?"

"Mr. Kingsley lets me stay in a room in the stable and charges me nothing because I muck out the stalls for him. Mr. Beeson, who owns this saloon, gives me three meals a day because I sweep the floors for him. I have a good life."

Win smiled. "I guess you do at that," he said.

Chapter 11

WIN AND JOE HAD TAKEN ROOMS IN THE FRONT OF THE hotel. The next morning a series of loud popping noises woke Win from the soundest sleep he had enjoyed in days. Startled, he sat straight up in bed, slipped his pistol from the holster, which hung from the bedpost, then got to his feet, ready for any intrusion. There was another series of loud pops, followed by the high peal of a woman's laughter, then the sound of a brass band.

Win moved over to the window and pulled the curtain to one side as he looked down on the street. The street was full of men and women, all dressed in their most colorful finery. There seemed to be a parade of some sort in progress, led by the brass band and a troupe of acrobatic dancers, followed by a highly polished, brass fire-engine pumper. The smell of food cooking over open fires filled the soft morning air and Win decided he would go down to have breakfast and to see what was going on.

When he got downstairs, he saw Joe eating a sandwich of barbequed beef and biscuit as he watched the celebration.

"I see you found the food," Win said.

Joe held up the biscuit. "This isn't bad. You ought to try it."

"Maybe I will," Win said, heading toward a stand that was selling sandwiches.

Smiling broadly, the sheriff came up to the two brothers then. "You'll like our barbeque," he said. "Folks from all over talk about how good Bertrand barbeque is.

"I haven't been keeping up with the date," Win said. "What's the occasion? Is it the Fourth of July?"

The sheriff laughed. "Fourth of July? Nope."

"Then what's the celebration?" he asked.

"Why, you and your brother are the cause of our celebration," the sheriff replied. "You mean you haven't figured that out yet?"

"What the hell are you talking about? How are we the cause of your celebration?"

"I take it you haven't gone down to look at the display on the porch of the general store," the sheriff said.

"No."

"Maybe you should. I think you will be proud."

Finishing their sandwiches, the two boys walked down toward the general store. There were men, women, and children standing around the front porch looking at whatever it was the sheriff said was displayed there.

"I'll be damned," Joe said when they were close enough to see the display.

There, in a pair of wooden coffins standing up against the wall, were the bodies of Billy Hooper and Marcus Scruggs. Though probably neither outlaw had ever worn a suit in life, they were both wearing new black suits in death. Their arms were crossed across their chest. Billy Hooper was holding a pistol in his right hand and nothing in his left. Scruggs clutched a pistol in his left hand and the knife he had thrown at Joe in his right. Hooper's eyes were closed, but Scruggs's were open, though the lid of his left eye was drooped half-closed. Scruggs's mouth was closed, but Hooper's mouth was open in what was almost a sardonic smile.

"It's the Bushwhackers!" someone shouted, noticing Win and Joe looking at the bodies.

"The Bushwhackers!"

"Three cheers for the Bushwhackers!" someone else called. "Hip, hip . . ."

"Hooray!"

"Hip, hip . . ."

"Hooray!"

"Hip, hip . . ."

"Hooray!"

Win held up his hand to silence them, then walked up for a closer look at a hand-lettered sign propped up at the foot of the coffins:

HERE ARE THE BODIES OF THE BANDITS
BILLY HOOPER AND MARCUS SCRUGGS, KILLED BY
THE BUSHWHACKERS
WIN AND JOE COULTER
THE GUNFIGHTS THAT KILLED THE TWO MEN TOOK PLACE
RIGHT HERE IN BERTRAND

"This is going to make our town very famous," someone said, and when Joe looked around, he saw the young boy who had stabled his horse for him the night before. "Of course, everyone knows that Billy Hooper wasn't really killed here, but we have his body, and the sheriff says that is the same thing."

"Is that what everyone thinks?" Joe asked. "That this is going to make Bertrand famous?"

"Yes," the boy answered. "The sheriff said that now everyone will come to see where the gunfights happened. They'll buy drinks and meals in the saloon and they'll stay in the hotel. The sheriff says everyone will get rich because of this."

"And that is what all this is about? This parade and picnic?"

"Yes," the boy replied. "The sheriff says we will have

•

such a celebration every year at this time. It would be nice if you could come every year."

"Sure. And maybe we could kill someone new for you next year," Win suggested.

"Do you think so? That would really be good," the boy said enthusiastically, not picking up on Win's sarcasm.

Win shook his head slowly, then nodded at his brother.

"Let's go," he said. "The sooner we could get out of this town, the better."

"For you boys, there is no charge," the liveryman said when Win and Joe reclaimed their horses. "You have made our town famous."

"And so, out of a sense of civic duty, you boarded our horses free?" Win asked.

The liveryman looked around, then said in a quieter voice, "Yes, but also I have taken Billy Hooper's horse. It will more than pay the bill."

"Yes, I'm sure it would," Joe said as the two brothers mounted and rode away.

There had been reaction to their killing before, especially during the war when they were able to extract vengeance for some of the more heinous atrocities. But never before had an entire town put their victims on public display and thrown a town party to celebrate. It was more than the boys could stomach, and they couldn't wait to shake the dust of this town from their feet. As soon as they reached the outer limits of town, they urged their horses into a trot, putting as much distance behind them as they could.

Chapter 12

BECKETT TRIED TO PISS A GRASSHOPPER OFF A WEED, BUT wasn't successful. He buttoned his trousers, then walked back over to the remains of the camp where he and Purcell had spent the night. There was a small pile of blackened twigs from the fire they had built the night before.

"You sure you told Scruggs where to meet us?" Purcell asked.

"Yeah," Beckett answered with a growl. "I told him."

"He's late."

"He's not late," Beckett said. "The dumb bastard isn't showing up. Hell, I should have known better than to count on him anyway."

"So, what do we do now?" Purcell asked.

"We'll pull the job by ourselves.

"You think we can do it? I mean, with just the two of us?" Purcell asked.

"Why the hell not?" Beckett replied. "Besides, this way, there will be more money for us."

"Yeah," Purcell said, smiling broadly. "Yeah, that's right, ain't it?"

"Let's go," Beckett said, walking toward the horses they had already saddled.

● ● ●

Dorena was a small town, just as Beckett had said. However, it was a busy town, and a half dozen wagons were parked along the streets. The board sidewalks were full of men, women, farmers, and ranchers, looking in the windows of the shops, hurrying to and fro.

"What the hell?" Purcell asked, surprised by the number of people. "Is this Saturday?"

"How the hell do I know? I don't keep no damn calendar," Beckett responded with a growl.

"Seems to me like they's an awful lot of people in town, Charley," Purcell said. "Maybe too many."

"Yeah?" Beckett answered. "Well, look at 'em. Most of 'em ain't even wearing guns. Don't worry about it."

"That looks like the bank over there," Purcell said, pointing to a rather flimsy-looking building. It was thrown together from rip-sawed lumber, and it was leaning so that it looked as if a good, stiff wind could knock it over.

"Hell, we don't have to rob this bank," Beckett said. "We can just kick the walls in."

"Let's do it and be gone," Purcell suggested.

"Wait a minute, wait a minute," Beckett said, holding up his hand. "Let's take a ride up and down the street first, just to get our bearings."

"What do you have in mind?"

"We'll ride down to the far end of the street and back. You take the left side. Count ever'body you see carryin' a gun. I'll take the right."

The two men rode slowly down the entire length of the town, then they turned their horses and rode back.

"I seen three that was wearing guns," Purcell said.

"I only seen one on my side," Beckett said. "What about the three you seen? Any of them look like they know how to use them?" Beckett asked.

Purcell laughed. "Nah. One old fart didn't look like he had the strength to even pull his gun out of the holster, let alone use it."

"Well, then, what do you say we get us a little travelin' money?"

Beckett and Purcell swung down from their horses, then wrapped the reins loosely over the hitching rail.

As soon as the two men were inside, they pulled their pistols.

"This is a holdup!" Beckett shouted. "You, teller, empty out your bank drawer and put all the money in a bag!"

Nervously, the teller began to reply, emptying his drawer in just a few seconds.

"Is that all there is? There can't be more'n a couple hundred there," Beckett said in disbelief.

"That's all there is," the teller insisted.

Beckett took the sack. "I want to see what you've got in the safe," he demanded.

"The hell you are! I just put my money in this bank, mister, and you ain't gettin' a cent of it!" a customer suddenly shouted. Beckett swung his gun toward the customer, who was also armed. The customer fired first. His bullet hit an inkwell on one of the tables, sending up a black spray of ink. Beckett returned fire, and his bullet found its mark. Purcell fired toward the teller's window, and his bullet shattered the shaded glass around the teller cages.

"Let's get the hell out of here!" Beckett shouted.

Outside the bank the townspeople, hearing the shots, realized at once what was going on.

"The bank!" someone shouted. "They're robbin' the bank!"

One of the armed townspeople started running toward the bank with his pistol drawn. Purcell, who was the first one out of the bank, shot him, dropping him in the middle of the street. Seeing that, the townspeople began screaming and running for cover.

Clutching the canvas bag in his left hand, Beckett fired

three more shots into the bank, knocking out the windows on both sides and in the door.

"Hurry! Get mounted!" Purcell called, holding the reins down for Beckett.

Across the street a young store clerk, no more than a boy, came running out of the store, wearing his apron and carrying a broom in one hand and a rifle in the other. He dropped the broom, raised the rifle, and fired. His shot hit Purcell in the side, and, with a roar of pain and anger, Purcell fired back, killing the boy. From the front porch of a hardware store, a man fired both barrels of a shotgun, but his gun was loaded with light birdshot and he was too far away to be effective. The pellets peppered and stung, but none of them penetrated the skin.

Another citizen had better luck, in that his bullet killed Beckett's horse. Beckett, with the bag of money in his hand, leaped from the saddle as his animal went down, then ran toward the nearest hitch rail. There, several horses were tied, left by their owners who had come into town. The horses were spooked by all the gunfire and they reared and pulled against their restraints.

Beckett grabbed the horse nearest him and swung into the saddle. When the owner stepped out the door of a nearby shop to protest, Beckett shot at him, and the bullet, hitting the door frame right beside the owner's head, drove him back inside.

The sheriff, an older man just as Beckett had described him, was now reaching the scene, having run the entire length of the street from the sheriff's office. He was carrying a rifle, and he raised it to his shoulders.

"You fellas stop right there!" he called.

"Would you look at that old fool?" Beckett said. He dropped the sheriff with a shot to the chest.

The two outlaws rode toward the end of town only to see a dozen or more of the townspeople rolling a wagon into the street. The townspeople then tipped the wagon over as a barricade and gathered behind it, all of them armed and ready.

"Charley, we can't go that way!" Purcell shouted.

"This way!" Beckett yelled, turning off the street and leading them through a churchyard where a funeral was in progress and the body was just being carried from the church.

At the sound of gunfire and the sight of mounted and armed men bearing down on them, the funeral procession broke up amidst screams and shouts of terror and outrage. The pallbearers dropped the coffin and the lid popped off, allowing the last remains of a bearded old man to roll out.

By the time the townspeople were able to regroup and get mounted, Beckett and Purcell had a two-mile lead on them. With the sheriff dead and no effective leader to organize them, the pursuit only lasted for a few miles. After that, the men gave up and came back to town to help calm the fears and bury the dead.

"They've stopped chasin' us," Beckett said, looking back over his shoulder. "We can give the animals a blow now."

They reined up, then swung down from their saddles and began walking their horses. Purcell, who had been hit in the hip, was walking with a painful limp. There was blood on the front of his trousers.

"You bad hit, Purcell?" Beckett asked solicitously.

"No."

"You sure? You're covered with blood and you got a pretty bad hitch-along in your get-about there."

"I ain't hurt bad," Purcell insisted. "I got a bullet in my hip, but it didn't hit none of my vitals."

"Yeah, well, we can't leave the bullet in there," Beckett said. "We'll have to get you to a doctor somewhere."

"No!" Purcell shouted. "I seen how you got a doctor for Mosley. I ain't plannin' on lettin' you leave me somewhere to die."

"That was different," Charley said. "We was on the run then."

"Well, what the hell, Charley? We ain't exactly goin' to a picnic now."

Beckett laughed. "That's the truth," he said. "All right, if you think you can keep up, come ahead. But you start slowin' me down any, I'm goin' to leave you."

"I didn't figure it would be any otherwise," Purcell replied.

"If you want, I can get that bullet out for you," Beckett offered.

"You a doctor, are you?"

"I've took out a few bullets in my day," Beckett said. "And some of 'em lived."

"I'll pass on that offer, but thanks just the same," Purcell said.

Despite Purcell's brave protestations, by nightfall the pain was almost unbearable, and he knew he wouldn't be able to go on unless the bullet was removed. He finally spoke the words.

"Charley," he said thickly. "You serious 'bout bein' able to take out a bullet?"

Beckett chuckled. "You ready for it to come out now, are you?"

"Yes."

"I thought you would be. I've heard 'em talk brave before, but most always they change their mind. I'll take it out for you."

"Thanks."

"It's goin' to cost you."

"Cost me? Cost me what?"

"Your share of the money we took from the bank."

"Are you crazy? I got shot for that money. You think I'm goin' to give it to you?"

"Don't look to me like you got no choice," Beckett said. "Anyhow, what's the big deal? We only got a little over two-hundred dollars. Your share's just one hundred bucks.''

"Who would've thought they would put up such a fight for just two-hundred dollars?'' Purcell asked.

"Do we have a deal?'' Beckett asked.

At that very moment a wave of nauseating pain swept over Purcell with such intensity that it was all he could do to stay in the saddle.

"All right, you bastard, all right, we have a deal. You can have my share, just get the damn bullet out,'' Purcell said in a strained voice.

"I know this country,'' Beckett said. "We'll head up into that draw over there. That'll take us into Snake Canyon. Maybe we can hole up for a while.''

"We're goin' to hole up?'' Purcell asked.

"That's right, Jimmy, we're goin' to hole up,'' Beckett said. He chuckled. "Did you really think I was goin' to leave you?''

"I don't know,'' Purcell answered. "Yeah, I guess I thought you might.''

"Well, I ain't. You an' me are the only ones left now. That means we got to stick together. Besides, what would folks think of Kansas Charley if they knew he abandoned his friends?''

"Yeah,'' Purcell replied, thinking of Ray Mosley, Kelly Sims, and Billy Hooper. "What would they think of you.''

It was another hour of painful riding before they stopped. Purcell climbed down from his horse, removed the saddle, then lay down, using it as a pillow. The pain which had been localized in his hip now spread throughout both legs and up his back.

"You need to build us a fire,'' Purcell said.

"Kind of hate to,'' Beckett replied. "You can see a fire a long way off at night. Somebody might see this and get to wonderin' who's out here.''

"You've got to have a fire so's you can heat the knife,'' Purcell said.

"All right, I'll build a little one," Beckett agreed.

Purcell, no longer having to fight to stay in the saddle, drifted in and out of consciousness. He was aware of Beckett gathering bits of mesquite wood, but he didn't see him actually start the fire. A few moments later, though, he did see the golden bubble of light in the night, with Beckett silhouetted against the flames.

Then he passed out again.

He woke up again when Beckett started actually digging for the bullet. The pain was excruciating, much more intense than it had been at any time before. He passed out again. When he came to the next time, Beckett was holding the bloodied bullet between his fingers and smiling broadly, his eyes and teeth glowing orange-red in the snapping fire.

"Can you believe this?" Beckett said. "This here is a .22. Who shot you anyway, Jimmy? Some kid with a toy gun?"

"I don't remember," Purcell replied, though, at that moment, he did recall that he had killed a young, apron-clad boy.

"Give me three of your bullets," Beckett said.

"What? What do you want my bullets for?"

"Because I need the gunpowder," Beckett replied. "And I ain't plannin' on usin' any of my own."

"I got a box of cartridges in my saddlebag," Purcell said. He tried to reach for them but was too weak.

"I'll get 'em," Beckett offered generously. When he opened the box he took out ten or twelve, dropping the extra cartridges into his own pocket. He came back to sit beside Purcell as he separated the bullets from the cartridges. When he had all three separated, he poured the powder on the wound.

"What's that for?" Purcell asked.

"You'll see," Beckett replied. Without a word of explanation, he picked up a burning brand from the fire and touched off the powder. It made a white-hot flash.

Purcell had time only for a gasp of pain before he passed out.

Chapter 13

WHEN PURCELL OPENED HIS EYES THE NEXT MORNING, HE was looking directly at the campfire, or rather, at what had been the campfire. Now there were only a few white coals with a tiny wisp of smoke curling up from the ashes.

"Charley," he said. "Charley, could I have a drink of water?"

When no one answered, Purcell turned, with a great effort, to look around. He didn't see anyone.

"Charley?" he shouted, the effort of the yell causing his wound to throb.

There was still no answer.

With a supreme effort, Purcell sat up and looked around. The camp was totally deserted. Not only was Beckett gone, but so were the horses. Beckett had left in the night, leaving Purcell wounded and without a mount.

"You son of a bitch!" Purcell shouted. "You bastard!" He picked up a rock and threw it, though the effort caused pain to shoot through him like a hot knife. He fell back down and lay there until the pain subsided somewhat. The thirst he had awakened with seemed to increase with his efforts, so he reached for his canteen. When he couldn't find it on his saddle pommel, he looked around for it.

The canteen was gone. So were his saddlebags. There

had been jerky, raisins, and dried beans in there. Beckett had taken his food and water as well.

Waves of panic swept over him, pushing aside the rage and even the pain. He was abandoned out there, no horse, too wounded to walk, and no food or water. He was going to die a long, slow, agonizing death. Even Ray Mosley had it better than this, he thought. He had food, water, and a place to sleep, followed by a quick death.

"Shit!" he shouted into the dry, morning wind. "I would have been better off lettin' them hang me."

Purcell saw his pistol and, in a sudden impulse, drew it from his holster. He put the barrel to his temple.

"Charley Beckett!" he shouted. "I'll be waiting for you in hell!"

He pulled the trigger.

At about that same moment, Win and Joe were pushing through the bat-wing doors of the Lucky Chance Saloon in the little town of Three Wells. Because it was a little early for the saloon's trade, it was relatively quiet. An empty beer mug and a half-full ashtray were placed conveniently by the piano to provide the only evidence that anyone ever played the instrument.

The boys ordered beer, and when it was served, Win turned around to survey the room as he drank it.

Two people were sitting at the table nearest the piano . . . a middle-aged cowboy and the only bar girl who was working at this hour. The fact that both of them had only one glass before them, and that the glass was still half-full, indicated that the bar girl either found the cowboy's company pleasant, or had accepted the slowness of the hour.

There were a few people sitting at one of the other tables as well, and a lively card game was in progress. The table was crowded with brightly colored poker chips and empty beer mugs. There were two brass spittoons within spitting distance of the players, but despite their presence, the floor was riddled with expectorated tobacco quids and chewed cigar butts.

Suddenly one of the players threw his cards on the table in disgust, then stood up. "I've had it, boys," he said. "I ain't drawed a winnin' hand since I sat down."

One of the players looked over toward the bar and saw Win watching them.

"We have an empty chair here, mister, if you'd care to sit in."

Win looked at Joe.

"Go ahead," Joe said. "Hell, you never have been able to resist a good poker game."

Win tossed the rest of his drink down, then wiped the back of his hand across his mouth. Joe was right when he said Win enjoyed a poker game. But he also knew that it was sometimes easier to pick up information through casual conversation over a few drinks and a deck of cards than to ask outright. Maybe someone at the table had heard something about Beckett.

"Thanks for the invite," Win said. "I reckon I will join you if you don't mind."

"What you take out of your pocket and put in front of you is all the money you can play with," one of the men said. "You can't go back for more."

"And you can't put anymore in front of you than the most any one of us have showing," another added.

"Sounds fair," Win said, looking around the table. Who's been the winner so far?"

"That'd be the doc, here," one of the cowboys said. "You'd better watch out for him. He's pretty good at the game."

"Thanks for the warning. And you would be the doc?" Win asked, addressing the man with the largest pile of money.

"I am," the tall, thin, cadaverous-looking man replied. He was wearing a black suit, a shoestring tie, and a flat-crown black hat. He counted the money in front of him. "I've got forty-five dollars here."

Win bought forty-five dollars worth of chips and stacked them up in front of him.

"You two boys just passin' through Three Wells?" the man in black asked as he dealt the cards. It was easy to see why he was ahead. He handled the cards easily, gracefully, whereas the others around the table looked awkward even picking up the pasteboards.

"My brother is," Win answered, nodding toward Joe, who had just ordered a second beer. "But for me, it depends."

"On what?" one of the other men asked, curious about Win's comment.

"It depends on how much I win here," Win answered. "If I win enough money, I might just settle down, right here in Three Wells. I'll buy a ranch and some cattle, get married, raise a family, join a church, run for the city council, and become a substantial citizen."

The men around the table laughed out loud.

"Say, Smokey," Doc called to the cowboy who was sitting with the bar girl. "Did you hear this fella? If he wins big, he's goin' to be lookin' for a wife. You better hang on to Belle while you can."

Belle looked over at Win. "Honey, you're a good lookin' man," she teased. "You wouldn't have to win too much to get me."

Belle's good-natured response brought more laughter.

Win won the first hand.

"Better watch it, Doc," one of the cowboys said. "This fella's on his way."

The game continued for several hands. Win was winning a little more than he was losing, but he wasn't the big winner. But neither was Doc. Win's entrance into the game seemed somehow to change the dynamics so that everyone's luck improved slightly. That had the effect of improving the corporate mood, and the talk came freely.

Besides Dr. Shelby, who was a real doctor in addition to being an almost professional gambler, the other men in the game were Mitch McCoy, a small rancher, Rank Feeler, a gunsmith, and Andy Potter, who owned the feed and seed store.

"Say," Win said as if merely taking part in the conversation, "did any of you fellas hear about the big jailbreak they had over in Commerce a few weeks ago?"

"Jailbreak? Mister, that's old news. Where you been?" Mitch replied. "Hell, yesterday, Charley Beckett and another man robbed 'em a bank over in Dorena."

"Some bank robbery," Rank said in disgust. "They only made off with two hundred dollars."

"They didn't get much money, that's true," Andy agreed. "But they killed some folks doin' it. And one of 'em was just a boy."

"A boy?" Doc asked. "What boy? I've doctored a few of the younguns over there."

"It was Muley Simpson's boy," Andy replied. "Muley runs the general store there, you know, and his boy was workin' for him. Seems the boy had just got hisself a new .22 rifle, an' when all the shootin' started, why he run out onto the front porch an' joined in the melee. They say he hit one of 'em, though they might just be sayin' that to ease Muley's pain some. Whether he actual did hit one of them or not, he got their attention, 'cause he was shot dead right there on the front porch of his pa's store."

"That's a damned shame. It's too bad they didn't get all them fellas hung when they had the chance," Rank said. "I wonder where they are now?"

"Say, you know I was talkin' to one of my nighthawks just 'afore sunup this mornin'," Mitch said. "Well, it was Pete Malloy. You fellas all know him. Anyhow, I was talkin' to him an' he said that last night he thought he saw a campfire down in Snake Canyon. I didn't put much store in it at the time, but now that I think back on it, don't it seem to you a little curious? I mean why would anyone want to go in there? The place is so desolate that a hawk has to carry a lunch just to fly over."

The others laughed.

"Snake Canyon, eh?" Rank said. "You think maybe Beckett is holed up there?"

"Well, if I was on the run, that's sure where I'd go," Mitch said. "Why, they's draws and gullies enough in that place to hide a whole army."

Over at the bar, Joe listened with half an ear to the dialogue going on around the table, while carrying on a simultaneous conversation with the bartender. At the same time, he was keeping an eye on Belle and the cowboy she was drinking with. He wanted to get closer to Belle, but he didn't want to move in on the cowboy. After a few more minutes the cowboy stood up, nodded to Belle, then stepped over to the bar.

"I reckon she's all yours, mister," he said.

"I don't want to rush you," Joe replied.

"Hell, mister, if I stayed all night, I couldn't do no more'n look at her over a half-empty glass. Belle's a nice girl, but she's a workin' girl, if you know what I mean."

"I know what you mean," Joe said. Joe turned to the bartender. "Give my friend here a beer, and send another drink over to the lady's table."

The cowboy smiled, broadly. "Mister, you are all right in my book."

Joe walked over to Belle's table. "Would you like some company?" he asked, pulling out the chair.

"Do you really want to sit here?" Belle asked. She leaned forward, showing a generous spill of her breasts. "Or, would you rather go to where it is more comfortable?"

"You know of such a place?"

Belle raised her eyes, glancing toward the second floor. "I have a nice room up there," she said. "If you are interested. And . . . if you can afford it," she added.

Joe chuckled. "I'm interested, and I can afford it," he said, offering her his arm.

With a broad smile, Belle stood up and stuck her arm through his.

"Ed!" Belle called, holding her hand out toward the bartender as they walked by the corner of the bar. The one word was all she needed. Knowing what she wanted, Ed handed her a full bottle.

"Belle, you're my kind of girl," Joe said as they started up the stairs arm in arm.

As they went up the stairs, they passed one of the girls who was coming down, just then starting her workday.

"Sue, do me a favor and have a drink with Smokey, will you?" Belle asked. "He's a little blue tonight."

"What's Smokey got to be blue about?"

"His dog died."

Sue looked sad. "Oh, that's a shame. I know what a store he set by that dog."

Joe looked back down toward bar and at the old cowboy. Smokey was carefully nursing the beer Joe had bought for him.

"Here," Joe said, taking out a couple of dollars. "Sit with him as long as this lasts."

Sue smiled and took the money. "You've got a deal, mister," she said.

Upstairs, Belle unlocked the door to her room, then pushed it open. Joe looked around. It was a typical whore's room, decorated in a way that combined the fact that it was both the whore's home and place of business. The bedcover was white with a great red heart in the middle.

"Nice," Joe said, indicating the bedspread.

"Thanks. I made it myself," Belle replied. "But, I didn't know you come up here to talk quiltin'."

When Joe looked back toward her, he saw that she had already stepped out of her dress. She was wearing nothing underneath.

Joe undressed quickly, then, with no further words passing between them, they were in bed.

Joe moved on top of her as her legs went around his waist and her hands moved down to help him make the connection. Joe lunged hot, hard, and deep. She moaned and writhed and raked his back with long fingernails. He looked down at her as he continued to rock against her, watching the reaction in her face, with every thrust. Her head rocked from side to side, her eyes were half-closed, and her lower lip was caught between her teeth.

Then, Belle tightened her legs around him, locking her ankles across his back. She clutched the bed for leverage and began pumping her hips hard against him until she exploded in orgasm.

Joe, who had waited for her, now let himself go as well. Through the blood pounding in his own ears, he heard her wild cries as he spent himself inside her, lunging and thrusting in a long final frenzy. He felt her hands snake up around his neck, felt her breasts heaving against his chest, felt her final convulsive shudder, then all was still.

They lay on the bed for a long time, breathing hard, as a faint breeze stirred the curtains at the open window.

"Well, now, I must apologize," Belle said.

"Apologize for what?"

"I . . . I don't often lose control of myself like that," she said. "I was positively wild. What you must think of me."

Joe laughed.

"What is it?"

"Darlin', we came up here to do this, didn't we? What do I think of you? I think you are a woman who loves her work and is very good at what she does."

Belle brushed a sweat-plastered fall of hair back from her forehead.

"Well I . . . I take that as a compliment," she said.

The saloon, which had been fairly quiet when Joe and Belle climbed the stairs, was beginning to fill up. It was crowded and noisy. Three of the most noticeable of the newly arrived customers were young men who wore their guns strapped low. They were louder and more boisterous than anyone else in the establishment, and they made a place for themselves at the bar by elbowing others out of the way. Occasionally one of them would get off a joke at someone else's expense, and he and the two with him would laugh uproariously at his cleverness, unaware or unconcerned that the rest of the people in the saloon were not laughing with them, but were instead taking it all in, in embarrassed silence.

"Who are the funny boys?" Win asked Mitch.

"The one with blond hair and the loudest mouth is Mel Butrum. He's the oldest. The one with the red hair is Willie Cole. The one with the dark hair and mustache is Eddie Webber. They rode for me once, 'til I got rid of them. Then they rode for one rancher after another 'til, one by one ever'one got sick of 'em. I guess they been fired by near 'bou ever' spread within fifty miles. Now they mostly drift about, rounding up a few strays for their money."

"Yeah, and sometimes the strays ain't even strayed off yet," Doc said. "What gets me is why none of the ranchers know that."

"We know it," Mitch admitted. "But we figure payin' a few bucks to get our strays back, is better'n havin' 'em rustled."

"They're a rowdy bunch of bullies, all right," Doc said. "Don't nobody like 'em. In fact, I'm a little surprised to see them. They got drunk here two, maybe three weeks ago and tore up the place. Sheriff Pratt told them they was either goin' to have to pay for the damages or spend thirty days in jail."

"Which did they do?" Andy asked.

"Hell, they didn't do neither one," Doc replied. "They just lit out. This is the first time they've been back since."

"I wonder if the sheriff knows they're in town?" Rank asked.

The three men, perhaps sensing that they were the subject of conversation, left the bar and wandered over to the card game.

"Well, now, this here looks like a friendly game," the one called Mel said. "Any of you 'bout ready to give up your seats?"

No one answered.

"Hey, you," Mel said to Win. Willie and Eddie laughed. "Why don't you take a rest for a while and let one of us sit in the game?"

"Hey, Mel, you want to play you go right ahead," Willie said. "I didn't come into town to play no cards. Hell, we can do that out at the bunkhouse. I come for somethin' else."

"Yeah, Willie, we know what you come for," Eddie said. "You come to dip your wick."

The three men found that enormously funny.

"So, how 'bout it. You goin' to get up, or what?" Willie asked.

"I'm not ready to quit yet," Win said.

"Is that so? Well, maybe if you'd win one big hand, you'd be ready," Mel suggested. "I'll help you." He started walking around the table. "Doc, here, has hisself a pair of jacks," he said. "Mitch is holdin' a king, queen, and ace, but no pair. Andy has a pair of tens." He stepped behind the gunsmith's chair. "Whooowee. Now, Rank has two kings." Mel looked up. "Hope you can beat two kings."

Doc, Mitch, Andy, and Rank groaned, and Win laid his cards faceup on the table. He had two Aces. "What do you say we leave the pot and deal again?" he suggested to the others.

"Thanks. That's damned decent of you," Doc said.

"Hold it now. That's no way to be. I'm just trying to help."

Win glared at the young cowboy. "I've had a belly full of you, mister," he said. "Back away from the table."

Win's words were cold and clipped, and the easy banter fell away from the three young men. Mel licked his lips, the tip of his tongue darting out, snakelike.

"What did you say to me?"

"I told you to back away from the table."

"Mister, you don't think you can make words like that stick, do you?"

"I reckon I can."

"I don't know why I'm wastin' my time explainin' things to a dried-up old bastard like you. Maybe I'm just an all-around nice guy. But maybe someone ought to tell you that when you're sittin' down and I'm standin' up, there's no way you can get a gun out faster'n me. Now, you goin' to back up them words? Or you goin' to eat 'em?"

"I reckon I'll back 'em up," Win said. During the entire confrontation, one of his hands had been under the table. Now he brought it above the table and everyone gasped, because he was holding a Colt .44. Win moved his lips into what could be called a smile, though the smile didn't quite reach the cold glint of his steel-blue eyes. "Looks like I did get it out faster, doesn't it? Now, you can try me, or you can go on about your business and leave us to ours."

The expression on the young cowboy's face changed from one of cockiness to fear. He put both hands up and started backing away.

"Listen, listen, mister," he said. "I didn't mean nothin' by all this. I was just funnin', that's all. You boys go on now and enjoy your game."

"We intend to," Win said.

The three cowboys walked away from the table.

Doc laughed. "Mister, if you won every hand for the rest of the night it would be worth it," he said. "I've been wanting to see somebody stand up to those boys."

Chapter 14

THE THREE COWBOYS STOOD DRINKING AT THE BAR. THEY were considerably more subdued than they had been when they first came in. Mel was drinking hard, tossing one whiskey down after another, while Willie and Eddie tried to calm him down. Finally, Willie and Eddie gave up and left Mel to brood, while they walked over to a table occupied by Sue and Smokey.

Although Joe had paid Sue to drink with Smokey, it wasn't something she minded doing. She, like all the girls in the Lucky Chance, liked Smokey. Nobody knew exactly how old he was, but it was said that he could remember the Alamo. It wasn't all that difficult for him to remember it. . . . His father was one of the brave men who had died defending it.

"Hello, Sue," Willie said.

Sue looked at him, then turned back to talk to Smokey.

"Hey, Willie, what do you think? It looks like Sue don't love you no more," Eddie suggested.

"Yeah? Well, we'll see about that," Willie retorted. "Look here, you old fart," he said to Smokey. "If you ain't goin' to take Sue up to her room for a little fun, then quit chewin' her ears off and let someone do it who's still young enough to get the job done."

Smokey turned in his chair and looked up at Willie. "You go ahead, sonny," he said. "Take her upstairs. I'll still be here when she's finished."

"Go ahead, Willie. You got his permission," Eddie teased.

"Yeah, well I don't need the son of a bitch's permission," Willie replied. He reached down to grab Sue's arm, and she had to stand quickly to keep him from pulling her to her feet. "Tell you what, Smokey. Why don't you go back over there and have a drink with Mel? This here ain't goin' to take very long."

Smokey chuckled. "No," he said. "I don't reckon it will."

"What's that s'posed to mean?" Willie growled.

"Why, it don't mean nothin', Willie," Smokey said. "I was just makin' conversation, that's all."

Willie laughed a high-pitched laugh. "Yeah, well, seem's that's 'bout all you're good for," he said. Tugging roughly on Sue's arm, he pulled her over to the stairs, then started pushing her up to the second floor.

"I feel sorry for the girl," Rank said.

Doc looked up. "Yeah, well, don't worry none about Sue. She's had plenty of experience handling people like that."

Though Win said nothing, he tended to agree with Doc. He didn't like to see any woman, even a soiled dove, mistreated, but it had been his observation over the years that women like Sue were pretty good at protecting themselves.

Win lost this hand, then pushed away from the table.

"I appreciate the game, gentlemen," he said. "But I think I'll just have a drink or two, then call it a night. Thanks for letting me sit in."

"We enjoyed your company, mister. New blood's always welcome if it's friendly," Doc said. "What about it, Rank? Another deal?"

"Not for me, thanks," Rank replied. "I think I'll call it a night too."

"Me too," Mitch added. "We may as well break up the game now or Mel will be over here again wantin' to play."

"Yeah, I'll go along with that," Andy said.

"You fellas can quit if you want to, but I'd like to get the winning edge back," Doc said. "There are a couple of other games going on now. I think I'll see if I can join one of them."

Win said good-bye to his new friends, then walked over to the bar and ordered a drink. He had taken only one sip when the bat-wing doors swung open and a man wearing a badge stepped into the saloon.

"It's Sheriff Pratt," someone said.

"Smoke's goin' to fly now, fellas," another put in. "He done give them three boys the word not to come back to town 'till they paid off the damages.

"Mel Butrum," Sheriff Pratt called.

"Hello, Pratt. What got you away from your coffee and your nice cushioned chair?"

"I smelled a stink in the air and I figured you was over here," Sheriff Pratt replied. "Did you bring one-hundred dollars to cover the damages you caused the other night?"

"I told you I wasn't goin' to pay for them damages," Mel said without turning around.

"Then I reckon you'll be spendin' some time in jail."

Mel and Eddie both turned toward the sheriff. Mel smiled evilly at him.

"I don't reckon I'd care to do that, Pratt," Mel said. "You see, I'm pretty much what you'd call an outdoors man. Gettin' locked up in a jail ain't for me."

Sheriff Pratt held out his hand. "Give me your gun, Mel," he said. "You too, Eddie."

Mel shook his head, the evil smile still pasted across his mouth.

"You want our guns, sheriff, you're goin' to have to take 'em away from us. That is, if you think you're able to do it."

At Mel's challenging words there was a sudden frenzied

movement as people in the line of fire hurried to get out of the way. Only Mel and Eddie remained at the bar. Even Win moved to the far end to be out of the way of any wild shot, should shooting break out.

"It doesn't have to be this way, boys," the sheriff said. "A few broken windows and chairs? It hardly seem worth dyin' over."

"That all depends on who's goin' to be doin' the dyin'," Mel said, moving his hand in position just over the handle of his pistol. "You see, the way I'm figurin' is, it ain't goin' to be me."

Win was a little surprised by Mel's bravado. He had already proven himself to be a braggart and a loudmouth, but when it came right down to it, braggarts and loudmouths usually caved in to calm courage. And this sheriff had already impressed Win with the fact that he was a no-nonsense, courageous man. What, then, was giving Mel his edge?

Win sensed, more than saw or heard, the movement at the top of the stairs. When he looked up, he saw Willie aiming at the sheriff. So, this was why Mel was so confident. He knew that Willie was upstairs with the drop on the sheriff, while the sheriff had no idea of the additional threat.

Ordinarily, Win would never interfere in another man's fight. There were many reasons why he stayed out of them. Most of the time people resented interference, even if it had been undertaken with the best of intentions. Other times he just didn't know which side to back. This time, however, he had no problem in deciding. He had met the three cowboys and already disliked them enough to be partial to anyone who might be opposed to them. As it turned out, that was all the justification he needed to give the warning.

"Sheriff, there's a man on the landing with the drop on you," Win warned loudly.

Angry that his ambush plans were spoiled by Win's yell, Willie turned his gun on Win.

"You son of a bitch!" he shouted, pulling the trigger even as he yelled.

Win jumped to one side, pulling his pistol and shooting almost as quickly as Willie. The slug that Willie fired from the balcony missed Win and slammed into the glass mirror behind the bar. The mirror shattered and fell, leaving only a few jagged shards hanging in place to reflect, in distorted images, the scene playing before it.

Willie didn't get away a second shot because Win had fired right on top of him, and Win's bullet found its mark. Willie dropped his pistol and grabbed his throat, then stood there, clutching his neck, as blood oozed between his fingers. Then his eyes rolled up into his head, and he twisted and fell, sliding head first down the stairs and following his clattering pistol all the way to the bottom. He lay motionless on the lowest step, his open but sightless eyes staring vacantly at the ceiling.

Win was still watching Willie slide down the stairs when he heard the roar of two more Colts. Though it seemed to him that time had stilled, thus causing a great separation between his and Willie's shots, and the next two shots, the truth was that the battle between Mel and the sheriff had taken place almost simultaneously with his own fight.

Mel had fired at the sheriff first, but his shot was badly placed. All it did was put a hole in the sheriff's hat. The sheriff's shot hit Mel in the forehead and Mel slid down to the floor in the sitting position, his body held up by the bar, his hands lying on the floor to each side of him. Like Willie, Mel had been killed instantly.

"No, no, don't shoot! Don't shoot!" Eddie shouted, holding his hands up in the air. "I ain't in this fight! I ain't in this fight!"

"Shuck your belt," the sheriff ordered.

"I'm doin' it, I'm doin' it," Eddie said, using his left hand to unfasten his belt buckle. The gun belt dropped to the floor with a clatter.

The sheriff looked at Eddie for a long moment, and Win

thought he was going to shoot him anyway. Finally he sighed, and made a waving motion with his pistol.

"Get out of here, Eddie," the sheriff said. "Just thank God you got out of here alive. Leave town and don't ever come back."

"But Mel and Willie," Eddie said, looking at two dead bodies with a sweep of his eyes.

"We'll take care of the dead," the sheriff promised. "Now, if you don't want to wind up in jail for a very long time . . . get out of here."

"I'm goin', I'm goin'," Eddie said, starting for the door.

The sheriff looked toward Win, then put his pistol away. Win did the same.

"I owe you my thanks, mister," he said.

"Yeah, well, I didn't plan to get involved," Win said. "But he didn't leave me much choice."

The sheriff looked at Win, then up toward the top of the stairs where Willie had been standing. He saw someone there holding a gun, and his hand dipped toward his own pistol.

"No, sheriff!" Win called. "It's all right! He's my brother!"

The sheriff nodded, then relaxed.

"That's a pretty good shot, you made, mister," the sheriff said to Win. "I'd say it was better'n sixty feet. Would you agree?"

"That's as good a guess as any," Andy said.

"It's seventy-five feet if it's an inch," Doc insisted.

The sheriff had gone over to Willie and was now examining the cowboy's wound. He didn't need to examine Mel. With a hole in his forehead, his eyes wide open and opaque, and in the sitting position, leaning back against the bar, Mel was very obviously dead.

"Seventy-five feet," Doc added, "and the bullet caught old Willie-boy here, right in the windpipe. Yes, sir, I'd say that was one hell of a shot."

The sheriff studied Win for a moment, then he looked

up at Joe. "Say, I know you boys, don't I?"

"I don't believe we've had the pleasure," Win replied.

"You're right, we've never met in person," the sheriff agreed. He shook his finger slightly as he pointed it at Win. But there's no need for us to have met for me to know who you are. You and your brother are the ones they call the Bushwhackers. I've had paper on both of you."

Win shook his head. "Far as I know, Sheriff, we aren't wanted out here."

"This was when I was sheriffin' back in Kansas."

"You're from Kansas?"

"That's right," the sheriff said.

"I reckon that sort of makes us natural enemies," Win said.

Sheriff Pratt rubbed his chin for a moment, then shook his head. "Well, if we ever was enemies, we ain't no more," he said. "What you just done squares things in my book."

"Glad to hear it," Win said.

"What you two doin' here?" the sheriff asked.

"We're looking for someone."

"These fellas?"

Win looked over at the two bodies. By now, they had been picked up and laid out side by side on one of the longer tables. "No," he said. "They just happened to get in the way."

"Who are you after?"

"I think I can tell you that," Doc volunteered.

"Oh? And who would that be?" the sheriff asked.

"Unless I missed my guess, he's after Charley Beckett," Doc suggested to the sheriff. Then he looked directly at Win. "That was pretty slick of you, Win, to get into a card game with us just so you could get information," he added.

"I've learned that sometimes it's better to take the long way around," Win explained.

"I guess that's right most of the time," Doc replied. "But the truth is, there isn't a man here who doesn't want to see Charley Beckett get his due. In case you missed what we were saying while ago, a fire down in Snake Canyon this time of year is awfully curious.''

Pratt chuckled. ''Doc, do you know you're givin' away information that's worth fifteen-hundred dollars?''

''Fifteen-hundred-dollars? How do you figure?'' Doc asked.

''There's five-hundred dollars reward money out on Charley Beckett, Billy Hooper, Kelly Sims, and Jimmy Purcell,'' he said.

''Not Billy Hooper,'' Win said.

''Yeah, him too,'' the sheriff insisted. ''He's worth as much as either one of the other two fellas.''

''Not anymore. Hooper is dead,'' Win said, matter-of-factly.

''Dead? What happened to him?''

''I killed him,'' Joe said.

''That would explain it then,'' the sheriff said.

''Explain what?''

''Why there was only two men seen in the bank holdup over at Dorena. Witnesses swear that the only ones they saw were Beckett and Purcell. Maybe that's because that's all there were. But that only takes care of Billy Hooper. It leaves a fella to wonderin' where Kelly Sims might be.''

''They split up when we were tracking them,'' Win said. ''Hooper and one man, who I am now sure was Kelly Sims, went one way. Beckett and Purcell went another. Unfortunately, we went after the wrong pair. We caught up with Hooper. I wanted Beckett.''

''Why him, anymore than the others? They're all worth the same amount of money,'' the sheriff said.

''Because Beckett is the one we want,'' Joe said.

The sheriff nodded. ''You aren't in this for the money, are you?''

''Sheriff, we'd go after that son of a bitch if we had to pay the reward ourselves,'' Win said.

''Wait a minute,'' the sheriff said. ''I think I see it now.

You boys must've had a run-in with Beckett during the war.''

"Not quite,'' Win replied.

"What do you mean, 'not quite'?''

"What my brother means is, if we had run into Beckett during the war, he would be dead by now.''

"Yes,'' the sheriff said. "Well, as far as I'm concerned, whatever reason you have is your own business. Beckett is a murderer, and the quicker someone takes care of him, the better off everyone will be. So, if the knowledge that he may be poking around down in Snake Canyon is useful to you, then use it with my blessing.''

"Thanks,'' Win said. "I reckon we will be checking that place out.''

Win and Joe weren't the only one to hear the possible location of Kansas Charley Beckett. Eddie Webber had been run out of the saloon a few minutes earlier by the sheriff, but he hadn't actually gone anywhere. Right now he was standing in the shadows by the bat-wing doors, just outside the saloon. With his back to the wall and a small, two-shot sleeve-gun cradled in his raised right hand, Eddie planned to shoot the sheriff the moment he stepped outside.

However, as he listened, he began to have other plans. If Beckett was worth money to these men called the Bushwhackers, how much money would they be worth to Beckett?

The player at the card table hadn't been the only one who saw the campfire last night. Eddie, Willie, and Mel had seen it too. And not only did Eddie know where it was, he knew a shorter way to get there. If he could get to Beckett before the Bushwhackers and provide him with information as to when and where the two brothers would come for him, Beckett might be very grateful. He might even let him join up with him.

Chapter 15

EDDIE WAS PRETTY DEEP INTO THE CANYON AT THE MOUTH of Mckenzie Draw. Though there were literally dozens of draws and gullies in the canyon that would offer shelter, Mckenzie Draw was the only one that offered a way back out. If Beckett knew that as well, then this is where he would be.

Eddie stopped just outside the mouth of the draw, then climbed up onto a protruding finger and looked over into it. It was too dark to see anything, so he decided to wait until dawn. He was alone, and he didn't know how many men might be with Beckett. He had no desire to stumble into the camp in the middle of the night. That would be a good way to get himself killed.

When Eddie looked to the East he could see a faint streak of pearl-gray. It wouldn't be much longer, until it would be light enough for him to approach. He could afford to wait it out. If they would listen to him and believe him, they would still have time to prepare an ambush for the Bushwhackers.

Eddie pulled a strip of jerky from his saddlebag, chewed off a piece, then wrapped what remained in the soiled and greasy waxed paper he kept it in. He chewed it for several minutes and it seemed to get bigger and bigger in his mouth. He wanted to spit it out, but he figured he would need the sustenance, so he continued to work at it. He finally managed to get the last bit down, then he followed that with a swallow of water. He wished it was coffee, but he knew that starting a fire would be foolish, perhaps even fatal.

The night finally lifted, illuminating the canyon floor in a soft, coral light, though lingering shadows still hung in the corners and edges of the deeper draws. Eddie climbed up to the top of the protruding finger and looked down into Mckenzie Draw once more. This time he saw the camp, but he was surprised to see that there was only one person there. He thought there was supposed to be at least two of them, maybe three. Where were the others?''

"Oh, you clever bastards," he said quietly. "You're keeping two men on watch while one sleeps. That way nobody can sneak in on you."

He wondered, though, why they had not yet come in. He also wondered why the lone man in camp had not built a fire for their morning coffee. Maybe they were being cautious. Why weren't they cautious the other night? Every nighthawk within twenty miles had seen the fire then.

Eddie chuckled to himself as he thought of an old saying. He said it aloud. "You boys have done shut the barn door after the horse is gone," he said.

Eddie stood up, brushed his hands together, then started walking down the other side of the little hill, leading his horse into the campsite.

"Hello the camp!" he called, holding his arm out so that anyone watching could clearly see that he wasn't carrying a weapon. "Hello the camp! I'm a friend!"

No lookouts came in, nor did they even make their presence known.

"Mr. Beckett?" Eddie called. "Charley Beckett? My name is Eddie Webber. I've come to join you, if I may."

Still no answer, nor movement. Even the one person in the camp was still.

"Listen, I want to warn you. Them boys they call the Bushwhackers is on their way. Someone give 'em the information that you was out here. It wasn't me," he added. "I swear, it wasn't me. I just overheard, which is how come I'm here. What you shouldn't of done is build a fire at night. Them things can be seen for a long, long way."

Eddie was beginning to get a little disconcerted when no one answered.

"Mister, are you asleep? You can't be asleep. Hell, I done made more noise than a herd of cows comin' into this camp." By now Eddie was right over the supine figure, and he squatted down to touch him on the shoulder. "What's the matter with you?"

The man on the ground suddenly rolled over. Eddie saw a flash of movement, then felt the barrel of the man's pistol under his chin. He heard the hammer being cocked.

"Who are you?" the man asked.

"Eddie Webber, Eddie Webber," Eddie said in fright, backing away so quickly that he fell on his back. "Don't shoot! Don't shoot!"

The man sat up, though it seemed to be with some effort. He held his gun leveled toward Eddie. "What are you doing here?" he asked.

"I came to warn you and the others about a couple of boys they call the Bushwhackers."

The man with the gun laughed, then he winced with pain and put his hand down to his hip. That was when Eddie saw that the man's right leg was caked with dried blood.

"You're hurt?" he asked.

"Yeah. Some kid shot me with a .22." He laughed again, a dry, brittle laugh. "Can you believe that? Jimmy Purcell gettin' shot by a kid? With a .22? You got any water?"

"I got a canteen."

"Give me some water."

"I ain't got that much, but . . ."

"I said give me some water!" Purcell cocked his pistol.

"Sure thing, mister. Didn't say I wasn't goin' to give you none," Eddie said, reaching for his canteen. He tossed it to Purcell, and Purcell pulled the cork, then began drinking thirstily.

"You're Jimmy Purcell?"

"Yeah, that's me." Purcell said, taking the canteen down and squinting up at Eddie. "Who'd you say you was again?"

"My name is Eddie, Mr. Purcell. Eddie Webber."

"What are you doin' out here, Eddie?"

"Like I told you, I came to warn you fellas about the Bushwhackers."

"Why would you do that?"

"Well, for one thing, I don't like the sons of bitches very much," Eddie said. "One of 'em killed a friend of mine yesterday. And for another, I thought maybe you and Mr. Beckett would let me join up with you."

Purcell laughed again, another dry, brittle, laugh.

"You want to ride the outlaw trail do you, Eddie?" he asked.

"Yes."

"You're bold and brave to want to join that gallant band of brothers whose home is the wind and whose destiny is danger?"

"What?"

Purcell laughed heartily. "I got that from one of those dime novels some fool wrote about Charley Beckett. Beckett carries them with him, you know, and if he finds somebody who hasn't heard of him, he shows them the books."

"I never knew they wrote no books about Charley Beckett."

"You've never heard of Kansas Charley?"

"Sure, I've heard of him," Eddie said. "I just never knew anyone had wrote any books about him."

Purcell laughed again. "Charley won't like that," he said. "He sets a great store by those dime novels."

Eddie looked around nervously.

''Where is he?'' he asked. ''I thought you two was together.

''Let's see. Where would ol' Charley be by now?'' Purcell asked. By now I reckon he's watching the whores dance down in Aquilla.''

''Aquilla? That's a hundred miles south of here, near to the border.''

''That's the general idea,'' Purcell replied.

''But, what are you doin' here?'' Eddie looked around the campsite. ''Where's your horse?''

''You noticed that, did you? My horse is gone. He took it with him, along with my share of the money from the bank job in Dorena and my water and food.''

''Why did he leave you here like this?''

''I guess he thought I'd slow 'im down,'' Purcell said. ''Thanks for the water.'' He handed the canteen back to Eddie.

''Sure,'' Eddie said. As he was hooking the canteen back on the saddle, he saw a plume of dust in the distance, glowing brightly in the early morning sun.

''Someone's coming,'' he said.

''The Coulters?''

''It has to be,'' Eddie replied.

''You got a rifle?'' Purcell asked.

''Yeah, I have a rifle.''

''Tell you what you do. You tie your horse here, then you take your rifle and go over there, in those rocks and wait. I'll be the bait, you see. And when the Coulters come into the camp, you'll have a perfect bead on them.''

''Yeah,'' Eddie said. ''Yeah, that's a good idea.''

''Leave me your pistol,'' Purcell said.

''What?''

''Leave me your pistol.''

''What do you want with my pistol?''

''That's a .37, isn't it?''

''Yes.''

"Mine's a .44. I don't have no bullets, and what you got won't fit mine."

"You don't have any shells at all?"

"None," Eddie replied. He thought of the empty, metal click, last night, when in despair he had put the pistol to his temple and pulled the trigger. "I reckon Charley thought I wouldn't have no need for 'em out here. When he left, he took everything, even the shells that was already loaded into my gun."

"No bullets at all, huh?" Eddie smiled when he got the idea. "Well, I'll be damned."

Win and Joe stopped when they heard the shot, flat and low in the distance.

"Did you hear that?" Joe asked.

"Yeah, I heard it."

"They couldn't be shooting at us. We're too far away. So the question is, why did they shoot in the first place? They're just giving their position away."

"Could be that they know we're here and they're just lettin' us know they know," Win suggested.

"Maybe," Joe agreed.

"Well, come on, let's see this thing through."

As the brothers moved up the canyon floor, they stayed close to the wall, taking advantage of the rocks and protrusions, passing through apertures when possible, rather than going around or over the long fingers.

They moved cautiously to the top of a long promontory, then looked over to the other side. They saw a hobbled, saddled horse and Jimmy Purcell sitting nearby, holding a coffee cup and staring into the remains of a fire.

"There's one of them," Joe said. He started to move, but Win reached out and took his brother by the arm.

"Wait a minute, little brother," he said. "There's something wrong here."

"Yeah," Joe said, pulling back. "I see what you mean. It is kind of peculiar the way he's just sitting there. He hasn't taken a drink of his coffee, moved or even twitched.

"If that's coffee, where did it come from?" Win asked. "There's no pot anywhere, no smell of coffee in the air."

"And not the tiniest wisp of smoke from that fire," Joe added.

"Joe, I've got a gut instinct that Purcell is dead," Win said. "That was what the shot was."

"You think Beckett killed him?"

"Yeah. They said the kid who was killed in Dorena hit one of the robbers. I figure he was slowing Beckett down, so Beckett shot him, then left him here as a decoy."

"Wouldn't be the first time the bastard has turned on one of his own," Joe agreed.

The two men holstered their pistols, then started down into the camp.

Suddenly Win got an uneasy feeling. He could see one saddle on the ground beside the propped-up body of Jimmy Purcell, and another on the horse.

"Joe, something's wrong!" Win shouted. "There's one saddle too many here!"

At that moment a rifle cracked, and the bullet whistled by, taking off Win's hat and fluffing his hair. Both Win and Joe leaped down from their horses and dived to the ground. They began wriggling on their bellies toward a small rock outcropping, reaching it just as a second shot came so close that Win could hear the air pop as the bullet sped by.

When the brothers made it to the rocks, they raised up slowly and looked toward the sound of the shot. Win didn't see anyone, but he did see a little puff of white smoke drifting slowly to the East. He pointed to the smoke, then to Joe, and Joe nodded.

The wind was out of the West, which meant that the shooter had to be somewhat west of the smoke. Win shifted his eyes in that direction, then saw the crown of a hat, rising slowly above the rocks. He waited until he thought enough of the hat was visible to provide a target, then he shot. The hat went sailing away.

"You son of a bitch! You put a hole in my hat!"

"I meant to put a hole in your head," Win replied. He was puzzled by the voice. It wasn't Charley Beckett or Kelly Sims. Who was it?

The ambusher fired again. The bullet hit the rock right in front of Win, kicking up tiny pieces of rock and shreds of hot lead into his face before it whined away behind him. Win turned around and slid down into the ground, brushing the hot lead from his cheeks.

"Did I hit you?" the man called.

"Close, but no cigar," Win replied. "Who the hell are you?"

The man laughed. "You don't recognize me?" he asked. "All I can say is, you sure got yourself one hell of a short memory."

Win remembered now . . . not the name, but the voice.

"He was in the saloon last night," Joe said. "He was with the two who got themselves killed."

"That's right. The name's Eddie Webber, in case you forgot."

"Eddie Webber," Win said. "I'll try to remember that."

"You won't have to remember it too long," Eddie said. He fired again, coming incredibly close. Win realized then that Eddie Webber wasn't just another wild cowboy with a gun. He was very good with the rifle.

"I'll say this for you, Eddie Webber. You handle that rifle pretty well."

"Yeah," Eddie said. "Back in the saloon, last night, there wasn't no way I was goin' to go up against you or the sheriff with a pistol. But with a rifle, now, that's a different story. I've won the Fourth July rifle-shooting contest for the last five years running."

"That's pretty good," Win said.

"Yeah," Eddie replied. "Good enough I figure to go into a new business."

"Ridin' the outlaw trail's not that smart a move," Joe said.

"Outlaw trail? No way. I'm goin' over to the other side of the law. I aim to take Purcell in and collect on him, then I'm going after Beckett."

"You're going to be a bounty hunter?" Win asked.

"That's right," Eddie replied. "I come out here to join up with 'em, only I found Purcell here, all alone. The others had gone on to Aquilla without him. Me and Purcell got to talkin', and the next thing you know, I find out he's worth seven-hundred-fifty dollars. He wasn't lyin' to me, was he? He is worth seven-hundred-fifty dollars?"

"He wasn't lying," Win answered.

"Seven-hundred-fifty dollars. What do you know about that? That's a lot of money," Eddie said. "So I got to thinkin' about it. Why should I join up with these fellas and get a price on my head, when I could just kill 'em, 'n get the reward myself? So, I killed the son of a bitch."

"Seems like the reasonable thing to do," Win replied. To Joe, Win whispered, "Keep him talking."

During the entire conversation Win had been slipping out of his boots, pants, and shirt. Now he put them on the ground behind where he had taken cover, arranging them so that, at a casual glance from a distance, it would look as if he were there. Then, barefooted and half-naked, he put the blade of his knife between his teeth and slipped away.

"Eddie, can I ask you a question?" Joe called, as he watched his brother leave.

"Go ahead."

"If you really are going into the bounty-hunting business, why are you trying to kill us. We don't have any money on our heads."

"Well, let's look at it this way," Eddie replied. "You boys are going after Beckett. I heard you say so last night. If you find him before I do . . . you'll get the reward. I don't aim to let that happen."

"So, you are willing to kill us just to get us out of the way?" Joe asked.

"That's true," Eddie said. Almost instantly after saying the words, Eddie fired. Joe was just changing positions at that moment in order to relieve his back. The bullet from Eddie's rifle seared his cheek as it took out a chunk of flesh. Blood began running down the side of Joe's face. If he had not moved at that exact moment, he would be dead.

"Did I get you?" Eddie called.

"Hate to disappoint you," Joe called back. "But you missed me by a mile." Even as he was telling the lie, he was holding his handkerchief to his face to stop the bleeding.

After having gone some thirty yards, Win found himself in a narrow, twisting fissure that worked its way down the side of the canyon, passing fairly close to where Eddie had taken cover.

Win stepped into the fissure and, putting his bare feet and hands on either side, began climbing.

Eddie fired again and his bullet nicked the heel of Win's boot, knocking it back behind the rock.

"Ha!" Eddie shouted. "I'll just reckon that stung a mite, didn't it? That'll learn you to keep your foot out where I can see it."

Win continued to climb until he reached a ledge. Once there, he left the fissure and crawled out onto it. Then, on his stomach, he wriggled over to the edge and looked down. Eddie was no more than twenty yards below him. Eddie was peering around the side of a rock, looking toward the place where he had last seen Win and Joe.

"Hey, Coulters! How come you ain't shootin' back?" Eddie called. "You boys ain't out of shells are you? Course, if you was, I don't reckon you'd tell me. I mean, Jimmy Purcell told me an' look what it got 'im. He told me he was out of bullets and I shot him. Like you said, it seemed like the reasonable thing to do."

Eddie fired again.

"If you keep shooting at rocks, you're going to run out of bullets yourself," Win said easily.

Startled, Eddie turned around. The expression in his face reflected the shock of seeing Win, not only in a place totally different from where Eddie thought he was, but also because Win was naked, except for a pair of underbriefs.

"What the hell?" Eddie shouted, swinging his rifle around, while, at the same time, jacking in a new round.

Eddie got the lever down, but he never pulled it back up. Win's right arm whipped forward and the knife flashed once in the sun as it sped across the distance between the two men. It buried itself to the hilt in Eddie's chest, penetrating his heart and killing him even before he could fully realize what was happening to him.

Chapter 16

AQUILLA WAS ON THE AMERICAN SIDE OF THE BORDER, but there were far more Mexicans than Americans who lived there. The land was arid and too poor for farming or ranching, though many tried, and a few even managed to eke out a meager existence. There were some who searched for gold or silver, and though little of those commodities were found, enough nuggets turned up to hold out tantalizing prospects. Thus the hunt continued.

Despite the bleakness of its agricultural and mining prospects, Aquilla was, nevertheless, a bustling town. It saw a surprising amount of money flow through its half-dozen saloons, whorehouses, gaming establishments, cafes, and hotels. Outlaws fleeing south often used Aquilla for one last American fling. And since many of those same outlaws were fleeing from bank robberies or other sources of ill-gotten gains, money was in abundance. On the other hand, Mexicans just arriving in America would often spend their lifesavings in one afternoon, too ignorant of the exchange system to know they were being cheated.

Aquilla had a sheriff and two deputies. One wall in the sheriff's office was decorated with wanted posters from both sides of the border. However, neither Sheriff Blakemore nor his deputies had ever made any attempt to apprehend any the men on the Wanted posters. If they had tried, they would have incurred the immediate wrath of the town's business community, for outlaws on the run were the main source of income. As a result, a man who had a price on his head in Texas, Colorado, Wyoming, or some such place was just as welcome in Aquilla as any other traveler.

The outlaws were very aware of Sheriff Blakemore's policy toward wanted men, so they were always on their best behavior in his town and around him. In fact, some of them even became friends with him and the sheriff's "rogues' gallery" became somewhat well known throughout the Southwest for a most unique reason. Almost three-quarters of the wanted posters on the wall in the sheriff's office were autographed by the very outlaw whose face graced the dodger.

Beckett was very familiar with Aquilla, having been there many times before. But he wasn't the only one who knew about the town. Kelly Sims knew about it as well, and he was waiting in a little grove of cottonwood trees about a quarter of a mile out of town. The sun had already set when Sims saw Beckett riding by.

"Charley?" Sims called to him from the shadows.

"Sims!" Beckett answered in surprise. "What are you doin' here?"

Sims mounted, then rode out into the road to join Beckett. "I figured if you was still alive, you would wind up here," Sims answered. "So, I just waited."

"Yeah, well, as you can see, I'm still alive."

"Where's Purcell?" Sims asked.

"He didn't make it," Beckett replied.

"What happened?"

"Purcell and me . . . we tried to hold up a bank in Dorena. The whole damn town was layin' for us. We had to shoot our way out of the bank. Purcell got hit as we were ridin' out. He died on the trail a couple of days later. Wasn't nothin' I could do for him. What about Hooper?"

"Me 'n him split up," Sims said. "I figured maybe we'd meet up here, but I ain't seen hide nor hair of him since we took out on our own. I figure the Coulters musta got 'im."

"Prob'ly so," Beckett agreed.

"You say you an' Purcell held up a bank?"

"Yeah."

"Did you get 'ny money?"

Beckett thought of the nearly two-hundred dollars he had in his saddlebag. "We got about fifty dollars," he lied. "What about you? You got any money?"

"No more'n a couple bucks," Sims answered.

Beckett stuck his hand down in his pocket, then pulled out twenty dollars. "Here," he said.

"What's this?"

"Purcell's share. He won't be needin' it."

Sims was surprised. "Thanks, Charley."

"Come on, let's ride into town and get a drink," Beckett offered.

"You been in this town before?" Sims asked.

"Yeah, lots of times," Beckett replied.

"What about the sheriff?"

"Don't worry none about the sheriff. All you gotta do when we get there is keep your nose clean," Beckett told him. "And don't get in any fights."

"You don't need to worry about that. I plan to stay outta trouble."

"That's good."

"I hope they got somethin' to eat in this town, though. I'm gettin' hungry for somethin' more'n jerky and thirsty for somethin' more'n trail water."

"Well, you've come to the right place," Beckett said. "Aquilla is known for good food and good whiskey."

"I could also use me a woman."

Beckett chuckled. "Oh, yeah, Aquilla is known for its whores, too."

"Food, liquor, and whores," Sims repeated. "And I got

me twenty dollars. What else would a man need?''

"Maybe more money," Beckett suggested. "Twenty dollars ain't goin' to go very far here. The problem with this town is, don't nobody hardly come here,'cept if they're wanted. That means the town's got us by the balls, and they know it. Everything here costs two or three times more'n it costs anywhere else.''

"Hell, I don't care how much things cost. It's not like I'm planning' on buyin' me a shirt and a pair of boots.''

"It ain't just the merchants," Beckett explained. "Anywhere else in the country a man can get him a whore to share his bed for two dollars. Here, they want five dollars.''

"Would them whores be Mexican or American?" Sims asked.

"Both, I reckon. Why, does it matter?''

Sims chuckled. "Long as they spread their legs, it don't matter to me whether they be Americans or Mex.

Aquilla was dark except for the patches of light that spilled out into the street from the windows and doors of the cantinas. The town was noisy, as several guitars competed with each other for attention. A few people were singing, and in the back of one of the cantinas, a trumpet ran through several high trills. Laughter and loud voices filled the night air, and occasionally a gunshot would ring out, though the people knew instinctively that the gunshots were in boisterous fun and nothing more.

"Hey, fellas," a woman called down to them from an upstairs balcony as they rode by. She was leaning over the balcony bannister, wearing nothing but an undergarment, and it was cut low enough to expose the tops of enormous breasts. But her breasts were large because she was large. "Hey, fellas, why don't you come on up here?" she invited. "I'll take both of you on for the price of one.''

With her red hair, pasty-white complexion, and flat, twangy accent, she was definitely American.

"You want to give her a try?" Beckett asked.

Sims looked up at the woman, then laughed. "No, I

don't think so," he said. He rubbed his crotch. "You know, I think I'll get me a little black-eyed Mexican girl. I like them girls. Course, you got to be careful you don't get a in'jun. Sometimes it's hard to tell the difference. I got me a woman one time back in Arizona Territory . . . thought she was Mexican but she turned out to be in'jun. The only thing that pissed me off is she charged as much as a Mexican whore, and I don't think you ought to pay as much for a in'jun as you do a Mex. Course, you ought not to have to pay for any woman. Say, Beckett, you ever had a woman you didn't have to pay for?"

"Yeah," Beckett said.

"When? Where?"

Beckett recalled the young Pemberton girl he and Mendoza had raped. She was young, almost too young, but when they took her clothes off, he saw that she was beginning to shape up like a woman. He rubbed himself now, as he thought about it.

To be as young as she was, she had fought like a tiger. He finally had to knock her out so that, when he and Mendoza took her, she was as still as if she were dead.

Mendoza complained a little. He said he wanted more life in the women he had, but Beckett reminded him that any woman, even a woman who wasn't moving, was better than no woman at all.

When they were both finished with her, Beckett tried to bring her to, but she wouldn't wake up. He started jabbing her with his knife. He hadn't really intended for what happened next to happen. But for some reason he couldn't explain . . . seeing her dark, red blood stream across her milky-white, naked skin did something to him. Before he realized what he was doing, he was stabbing her, over and over again.

"You didn't have to kill her," Mendoza said. "If you'd'a kept her alive, we could'a had some more fun with her."

Beckett looked down at the young Pemberton girl's pu-

bescent body and at the trails of blood, drying now on her white skin.

"Ah, she was half-dead anyway," he finally said. He knelt beside her, then grabbed one of small breasts and began to carve.

"What are you doing?" Mendoza asked.

"I'm getting me a souvenir," Beckett said.

Beckett hacked off the girl's breast and took it with him. Then, after he got away from the Coulters in the night shootout at the monastery, he scraped the flesh out, dried the skin, and made it into a tobacco pouch. He had never actually used it as a tobacco pouch, though he did carry it with him.

"I've got her tit," he added matter of factly.

"You've got what?" Sims asked, surprised by Beckett's comment.

"You asked if I ever had me a woman I didn't pay for. I answered, yes, I did," Beckett said. "And I've got her tit."

"You've got her tit?"

"Yes. You want to see it?" He reached down into his pocket and pulled out a small, dry, leathery object and handed it over to Sims.

Sims, thinking it was a joke, took it from him. At first he was sure that it was leather, then he saw a little spongy protrusion and, curiously examined it more closely. Then suddenly he realized that the little piece of sponge was actually a nipple. When he realized that, he let out a little shout and threw it.

"Son of a bitch!" Sims shouted. "It really is a tit!"

"Goddamnit, what'd you throw it away for?" Beckett asked irritably. He got down from his horse and picked it up from the dirt, wiping it off before putting it back in his pocket.

"What the hell is the matter with you? You crazy? How

can you carry somethin' like that around with you?'' Sims asked.

Beckett laughed. ''What are you gettin' so upset about?'' Beckett asked. ''This here tit come off young, white-trash Secesh. Anyhow, where do you get off findin' fault with me? It ain't like you ain't never been a part of killin' a woman. You was there when we kilt the Doc's wife, and if you ever get caught, you are going to hang as high as me over that one.''

''Maybe so, but we didn't cut off her tit,'' Sims said.

''She wouldn't of felt it, if we had cut off her tit,'' Beckett said. ''Same as this girl. She didn't feel a thing. Come on, let's quit palavarin' and get to drinkin'.''

The drinking establishment was much more Mexican in flavor than American, even to the point that entry was through a clacking curtain of beaded strings, rather than through the more American, bat-wing doors. Inside, the bar was noisy with conversation, half of it in Spanish, half in English.

''Hello, Señor,'' a pretty, young Mexican girl said, coming up to Sims. ''I am very thirsty and I do not want to drink alone. You will drink with me?''

Sims started to reach for her, then he saw the top of her full, creamy breast spilling out over her low-cut blouse. He thought of the little piece of leather he had handled just a moment earlier and his blood ran cold. He turned away from her.

''No,'' he said. ''Go find someone else.''

''What the hell's the matter with you?'' Beckett asked, surprised by Sims's strange reaction. ''I thought you said you wanted some good-lookin' Mexican gal.''

''No . . . not now, not yet,'' Sims replied, not wanting to explain to Beckett why he was feeling like he was.

''Well if you don't want her, I do,'' Beckett said. He put his arm around the girl. ''Come on, honey. You want a drink, let's get a whole bottle and go upstairs.''

Of the two men, Beckett was clearly the least attractive

to the woman. In fact, there was something almost frightening about him. That was why she had made her initial overture to Sims. But he had refused, and she was in a business where she couldn't afford to be choosy. So she kept the disappointment hidden behind her eyes and pasted on a smile.

"All right," she said to Beckett. "If your friend does not want me, then I will go with you." Teasingly, she put her hand in Beckett's hair and twisted a strand of it around her finger. "If you want me," she added, coquettishly.

"Honey, you come with me and I'll show you just how much I want you," Beckett said, grabbing her and walking over to the bar to buy a bottle.

Sims watched Beckett and the Mexican girl take their bottle up the stairs, then he, too, walked over to the bar.

"Can I get anything to eat here?" he asked.

"Frijoles. Tamales," the bartender answered.

"Anything American?"

"Eggs, Señor."

"Steak?"

The bartender nodded. "Si, steak too."

"Fix me a steak and some eggs," Sims said. "And let me have a pitcher of beer."

"Si, Señor Sims. Anything you want," the bartender replied.

Sims looked surprised. "You know who I am? You recognize me?"

"No, but Señor Beckett called you Sims. Is that not your name, Señor?"

The smile left Sims's face. For a fleeting moment there, he thought he had achieved a degree of fame. "Yeah," he said, somewhat crestfallen. "Yeah, that's my name."

Chapter 17

KELLY SIMS TOOK THE PITCHER OF BEER FROM THE BAR-tender and walked over to a corner, where he found an empty table. He sat down with his back to the wall and began drinking his beer. Then he reached into his back pocket and pulled out a rolled-up dime novel and laid it on the table.

He had bought the dime novel long before he actually met Beckett. He wouldn't admit it to anyone . . . especially not to Beckett . . . but sometimes he secretly dreamed of the day someone would write a penny dreadful about him.

The pages were torn and the printing was getting dim from sweat, grime, and wear. The drawing on the cover was still discernible, however, and Sims studied it for a long time. It showed a man on a horse, fleeing before a posse. Hanging across the pommel of his saddle were two large bags, and if the reader couldn't figure out what the bags were, they were clearly marked by oversized dollar signs. A train was in the background. The door of the mail car was open and someone was standing in the opening, holding his fist over his head. A word-balloon from the mouth of the character said, "It's Kansas Charley! He has just robbed the express!"

There were several people leaning out of the open win-

dows of the cars on the train, and all of them seemed to be
armed and shooting at the fleeing robber. The robber, who
according to the book was Kansas Charley Beckett, was
holding the reins of his horse in his teeth while he was
twisted around in the saddle, firing both guns at the pur-
suing posse, two of whom were in the process of falling
from their saddles with mortal wounds inflicted by Kansas
Charley's unerring pistol fire.

The cover left unexplained how a posse managed to ar-
rive on the scene so quickly that the train Kansas Charley
had just robbed was still sitting on the tracks. It also did
not take into account the fact that, of all the crimes for
which the real Charley Beckett was charged with, none of
them involved robbing a train, which was in fact, much too
dangerous an operation for Charley to ever consider.

The name of the novel was: *Kansas Charley's Bold Midnight Robbery of the Denver Express,* though the robbery
depicted on the cover was very obviously taking place in
daylight.

Sims began to read:

*He came upon the train with both guns blazing and the
reins of his horse held in his teeth. "Stand and deliver!"
he shouted in a voice that was both heroic and frightening.*

Sims wondered how anyone could even talk with the reins
in his teeth, let alone sound off in a voice that was both
heroic and frightening. And though he had never used the
line "Stand and deliver," and he was pretty sure Beckett,
about whom this book was supposedly written, had never
used it either. But it did have a good ring to it and he
decided that in his very next holdup he would use it.

*"It is Kansas Charley," the engineer shouted to his fire-
man. His voice was laced with fear and respect, for Kansas
Charley was known throughout the West as the deadliest*

shot alive. It has been reliably reported that he can shoot the leg off a fly at fifty paces.

There was a shower of sparks and the squeal of steel wheels sliding upon steel rails as the frightened engineer brought his great iron steed to rest.

"Open the doors of the express car or feel the fury of hot lead!" Kansas Charley demanded.

Though the armed guards of the express car were filled with the greatest of trepidation, the ladies of the train, all of whom had hurried to the windows as a more opportune place from which to get a good look, were strangely devoid of fear. They seemed, instead, romantically smitten by the handsome young man who sat astride his horse, holding the brace of pistols leveled at the express car door.

A plate of steak and eggs was put on the table in front of Sims, but he was too absorbed in the story to bother to look up. He reached for the steak and picked it up in his hands.

"Sims, you really need to work on your table manners," Joe said. "Haven't you ever heard of a knife and fork?"

Gasping, Sims looked up to see that the person who had just delivered his food was not the bartender but Joe Coulter. Joe had his pistol out. He waved the end of the barrel.

"Go ahead, take a bite," he said. "I never liked to disturb a man before he was finished eatin' his supper."

Sims held the piece of meat just in front of his mouth, staring, wide-eyed at his captor.

"Go ahead, eat," Joe said again.

Sims raised the steak to his mouth, then, suddenly he dropped it and made a mad grab for his pistol. But Joe was quicker and he brought his pistol down hard on Sims's head. Sims fell like a poleaxed steer.

"You shouldn't read that trash, Sims," Joe said quietly. "You'll get to believing it."

Joe bent down to pick up Sims's pistol. Then he dragged Sims's limp, unconscious form over to one of the supporting posts, where he propped him, putting one arm to either side of the post. Then he tied Sims's hands together with a short piece of rope.

The guitar music, laughter, and conversation had all come to a stop when Joe knocked out Sims. Most of the other patrons looked on in curiosity, making no comment until they saw Joe put on the handcuffs.

"Hey, what the hell? You a lawman, mister? 'Cause if you are, you got no jurisdiction here," someone said.

Joe looked over at the speaker. "Who are you?" he asked.

"I'm the man that's goin' to teach you better than to come into Aquilla when you ain't wanted. Who the hell are you?"

"The name is Coulter. Joe Coulter," Joe said. He pointed to Win, who was standing just inside the door, with his pistol drawn. "That's my brother, Win."

The man who had issued the challenge, measured the look in the eyes of the two brothers and realized that he was about to make a big mistake. He began dissembling.

"Listen, you boys don't pay me no never mind," he said in a frightened, quivering voice. "You go on about your business . . . do whatever it is you come to Aquilla to do. You won't get no gruff from me."

"Well now, that's very nice of you," Joe replied. He walked back over to the table where Sims had been sitting. His untouched steak had fallen back onto his plate and Joe sat down and began eating it. He picked up the pitcher of beer and took several swallows before he set it back down. The rest of the saloon continued to watch him in silence.

"Play," Joe said to the guitarist.

"Sí, Señor," the guitarist said, and he began a heavy chording.

Win chuckled at his brother's confiscation of the unexpected meal. Then he walked over to the bar.

"There were two of 'em," Win said, holding up two fingers and indicating Sims, with a nod of his head.

"Sí, Señor."

"Where's the other one?"

The bartender didn't answer, but he did cut his eyes up.

"Thanks," Win replied.

Upstairs, in the girl's bedroom, Beckett had heard the saloon below grow strangely quiet. He stopped.

"Are you finished, Señor?" the girl asked.

"Shut up," Beckett hissed.

"*Que?*" the girl asked, surprised by Beckett's harsh command.

"I said shut up!" Beckett hissed again, putting his hand over her mouth. When he was sure she wouldn't speak again, he pulled his hand away. The girl took a long, gasping breath.

Beckett sat up and swung his legs over the side of the bed, then reached for his pistol. It was still deathly quiet below. "Don't you hear that?" Beckett asked.

"I hear nothing, Señor," the girl said in a quiet, whimpering voice.

"Yeah, that's just it," Beckett said. "Neither do I."

Still holding his pistol, Beckett began slipping back into his pants. He was already buttoning them up when the guitar music started again. Even this, however, was different. Before the music had been soft and melodious, a single-string melody weaving in and out of gentle chording. Now it was loud, syncopated, and invasive.

Beckett slipped into his boots and kept his eye on the doorknob. He just got them on when he saw the knob move ever so slightly.

Beckett began firing, punching a pattern of six bullets through the door in such a way that one of them was sure to be fatal for whoever was on the other side.

With an angry shout, Beckett rushed across the room and kicked open the door. He ran out onto the landing just outside the door.

• • •

Win actually had jiggled the doorknob then stepped to one side, no more than a second before the fusillade of bullets. He had stood with his back to the wall, watching the spray of splinters as the bullets came through. Then he had heard Beckett's loud, angry shout as the outlaw dashed across the room. When Beckett appeared on the landing Joe had brought his pistol crashing into the back of Beckett's head. The blow, plus the momentum of Beckett's rush, carried him through the bannister, causing him to crash, belly down, onto one of the tables in the room below.

By the time Win reached the bottom of the stairs, Sheriff Blakemore was stepping through the beaded curtains of the front door. He saw all the patrons of the saloon standing to one side or the other, giving Joe a lot of room.

"What the hell is goin' on here?" the sheriff asked.

"We have a couple of prisoners for you, Sheriff," Joe said. He pointed to Sims. "The one tied to the post is Kelly Sims. The other one is Kansas Charley Beckett."

The sheriff shook his head. "I got no call to hold them two fellas," he said. "They ain't done nothin' in my town."

"All we want you to do is to keep them overnight while we get a little sleep. They're both wanted men," he said. "My brother and I will be takin' 'em back with us in the morning, soon as we get a little rest."

"They may be wanted men where you come from, mister," the sheriff said. "But they ain't wanted here, and I'm not puttin' 'em in my jail."

By now Sims was conscious, and hearing the sheriff's refusal to cooperate, began to heckle Joe and Win.

"What are you two boys going to do now?" he asked. "Seems to me like you're 'bout the end of your rope." He giggled loudly.

"Don't worry about it, Sims," Win said. "The sheriff has just changed his mind. He is going to keep you two for us, after all."

"What the hell you talkin' about?" Sheriff Blakemore asked angrily. "I ain't changed my mind."

Win's draw was as quick as the flick of a rattler's tongue. He raised his pistol and pointed it at Sheriff Blakemore. "Sheriff, you can go down to the jailhouse as their jailer or their cell mate. The choice is yours."

"Suppose I don't like either choice?" the sheriff replied.

"There is a third choice," Win explained. "You can go out of here stretched out on that door." He cocked his pistol.

"I'm the sheriff. You wouldn't shoot me."

Win fired. His bullet clipped off a tiny piece of the sheriff's left earlobe, sending out a spray of blood. The sheriff, with a shout of pain and terror, slapped his hand to his ear. The wound was bleeding profusely and the blood began streaming through his fingers.

"You're . . . you're crazy!" the sheriff said.

Win moved the pistol to aim at the sheriff's other ear. Quickly, he covered it up.

"This time I'll take off a couple of fingers, too," Win suggested.

"No! No! Wait!" the sheriff said, holding his bloody hands, palm out toward Win. "Don't shoot again. I'll put 'em up for you!"

Win smiled and lowered his gun.

"I thank you for your cooperation," he said "Come first light in the mornin' my brother and I will be by for them."

Chapter 18

THE NEXT MORNING, A CROWING ROOSTER WOKE WIN JUST before first light. He sat up, stretched, pulled on his boots, then walked over to the chifferobe, where he poured water from a pitcher into a basin and splashed a little onto his face. He banged on the wall that separated his room from Joe's.

"Joe. Joe, wake up. Let's get goin'," he called.

"Yeah, yeah, I'm awake," Joe's muffled voice sounded through the wall.

A few minutes later Win and Joe tromped downstairs, past the snoring hotel clerk, and out into the early morning coolness.

The difference between Aquilla in the morning and Aquilla in the evening was like that of two towns. Last night the streets had been noisy with high-pitched laughter, boisterous song, loud talk, and banging guns, most discharged in fun, a few in anger. But even the most dedicated reveler was in bed now, and the only sounds to be heard were the sounds of the other half of the town . . . the working half . . . waking up.

There was the sound of the scrape, roll, and drop of cargo as a freight wagon was being loaded. They walked by a woman doing her wash, and Win could hear the scruffing of wet clothes being rubbed back and forth across a washboard. An early riser was doing some carpentry work, and Win heard the rip and tear of the saw-teeth, chewing into the piece of lumber, adding its noise to the morning cacophony.

Win woke the stableboy and paid the fare, not only for his and Joe's horses, but for Sims and Beckett's horses as well.

"At least the horses look ready," Joe said.

"That's good," Win replied. "I have no desire to have one of them break down on us."

The two brothers rode down to the far end of the street, leading the two empty, but saddled horses. The hollow sounding hoof beats echoed loudly off the walls of the storefronts.

"Curious, isn't it?" Win asked.

"What's curious?"

"How four horses can walk down a main street at high noon and barely be heard, and yet now the hoofbeats are so loud that I doubt we could make any more noise by banging on a drum."

They stopped in front of the sheriff's office and tied up at the hitching rail.

Inside the office, the sheriff was already up, sitting at his desk. He had a bandage tied all the way around his head, covering his shot-up ear. As a result he looked much more badly hurt than he was. He was drinking coffee and eating a biscuit, and he glared at Win and Joe.

"Good morning, Sheriff," Joe said, with exaggerated cheer. "I see you fixed breakfast."

"Not for you two, I didn't," the sheriff growled.

Joe walked over to the stove and lifted the coffeepot, then he opened the saver and looked inside at a full pan of biscuits.

"Uhmm, that sure smells good," Joe said.

"That's for my deputies," the sheriff said.

Win clinked a half-dollar down on the corner of the sher-iff's desk.

"Tell 'em to get their breakfast somewhere else," he ordered. He filled two cups, then grabbed four biscuits and started back to the cells. "Sims, Beckett, wake up," he called. "It's time to be goin'." He passed the coffee and biscuits through the bars.

"You poison this?" Sims asked.

"Now why would I poison you, Sims?" Win answered good naturedly. "If I didn't want to see you hang, I would've shot you last night. Besides, seein' as how you missed your supper, I figured you might be hungry this morning."

"Yeah," Sims said. "Yeah, that's right. I did miss my supper last night. What happened to it, anyway?"

"I ate it," Joe said, coming up to stand just outside the cell. He was eating a biscuit as well, which he devoured half of in one bite."

"The way you're wolfing that down, it's a wonder we're gettin' anything at all this mornin'," Sims complained.

Beckett took his breakfast without comment, and the two men returned to their bunk, where they sat down to eat.

"Don't get to thinking you're having breakfast at Del-monico's," Win told them. "Swallow that down pretty quick. I'm about to have a little breakfast of my own, and when I'm done, we're leavin' whether you're finished or not."

"Where you planning on takin' us?" Beckett asked.

"Back to Commerce, where we're going to watch you die."

"Hah! You think I'm going to hang?" Becket asked with a scoffing laugh.

"That's for the jury to decide," Win said.

"You damn right it is," Beckett said.. "And the jury's got nothing on me. I'm willin' to lay a bet, right here and now you ain't goin' to watch me hang."

Win smiled at Beckett, but the smile got no farther than

the spreading of his lips and the baring of his teeth. Such a smile did nothing to soften his countenance. Instead, it made him look even more menacing. "Oh, I may not watch you hang," Win said, "but, I will watch you die."

Beckett started to ask him what he meant, but he hesitated when realization dawned on him. Win Coulter was telling him that if the court didn't sentence him to die, he, Win Coulter, would. And he would also carry out the penalty . . . of that, Beckett had no doubt. He shivered, and Joe laughed.

"You know what it means, when you shiver like that, don't you?" he asked.

Beckett glared at him.

"It means, someone has just stepped on your grave."

Win walked over to the wall hook and took down the key ring.

"Coulter?" Blakemore called. Win stopped and looked toward the sheriff. Blakemore ran his hand through his hair, then adjusted the bandage around his head. "You two boys better keep an eye open," he said. "I heard some talk."

"What sort of talk?"

"Several of the boys got together last night," the sheriff said. "They may be planning some sort of a surprise for you."

"Really? I know there is supposed to be honor among thieves and all that, but I hardly think the likes of Kansas Charley Beckett can instill such loyalty or honor among his peers. Kelly Sims either, for that matter."

"They ain't doin' it for him or for Sims," the sheriff said. It's just that they figure if they can kill you two boys and free your prisoners, it'll be a sign to all the other bounty hunters and lawmen that Aquilla should be left alone."

"Thanks for the warning," Win said.

"I'll be honest with you. If they get the job done, I ain't goin' to lose no sleep over it," Blakemore said. "But bushwhackin' a man on the trail, that's goin' too far, even for me."

"Do you have any idea where this is supposed to happen?"

"No," Blakemore said. "I told you all I know. The rest is up to you."

Win and Joe rode behind Charley and Beckett, using their proven method of securing the two prisoners to each other and to him by hangman's nooses. To be honest, he wasn't one-hundred percent certain that the nooses would really break their necks if they attempted to run. That was because the fear the nooses instilled in his prisoners was great enough that no one had ever tried it.

They crossed a little stream, and Win watched the hooves kick up silver sprays of water as they went across.

"Hey," Beckett called. "Let's stop here for water."

"We've got enough water in our canteens," Win replied.

"The water in our canteens tastes like piss," Beckett said. "This will be good, cold water."

The swiftly running water in the stream was cool, and Win knew it would be good, and Beckett was right. The water in their canteens was tepid and sour. But if they stopped there, it might well be the last stop. That was because for some time now Win had been aware that three men were dogging them, riding parallel with them and, for the most part, staying out of sight. When he glanced over at Joe, he saw that his brother had noticed them as well. The two brothers nodded to each other, but they didn't say anything that would let their prisoners know that they knew they were being followed.

"We'll drink the water that's in our canteens," Win said.

The stream would have been a perfect spot for those who were following them to try their ambush if they were going to. Win didn't plan to give them that opportunity.

"I think my horse is going lame," Sims said a short while later.

"Do you?"

"Yeah, can't you see him? He's favorin' his left foreleg somethin' awful."

"What do you think, Joe? You're the one that's good with horses. Has Sims's horse come up lame?"

"Not that I can see," Joe said.

"Well, then you're blind," Sims said. "We've got to stop. We've got to stop, I tell you, and give him a rest. Maybe he's just picked up a stone or something."

"What do you think, Win?" Joe asked, quietly. "Both of them have tried to make us stop. Would you say they're trying to set up an ambush?"

"That's the way it appears to me, little brother," Win replied.

Win looked over to his left without being obvious about it, and saw three riders slipping through a notch in the hills, moving so quietly and expertly that only someone who was specifically looking for them would have noticed.

Ahead of them was a narrow draw. While they were in the draw they would be protected, but when they emerged from the other end they would be exposed.

"Win, there are some rocks just on the other side of the draw," Joe said, quietly. "If I was doin' the ambushin' instead of bein' ambushed, that's where I'd be waitin'."

"Yeah, that's pretty much the way I see it, too," Win replied.

As soon as they entered the draw, Win ordered them to stop.

"Stop? What for?" Sims replied. "If we're goin', let's go. No need to pussyfoot around about it."

"Well now, Sims, didn't you just tell us a while back that your horse was going lame. Here's your chance to take a look at him," Win suggested.

"Yeah, I know I said that, but I don't think it was anything," Sims replied. "I think he just picked up a small stone, then threw it, that's all. He's doin' fine now."

"Well, we'll stop anyway," Win said, giving a small jerk on the rope.

"All right, all right!" Sims complained. "But be careful with that rope, will you? You're goin' to break our necks if you don't watch out."

"No," Win said. "I'm goin' to break your neck if *you* don't watch out. Now, climb down."

The two prisoners climbed down, then Sims started to go through the motions of looking at his horse's hoof.

"Don't bother with that," Win said.

"What?"

"There's nothing wrong with your horse. You know it and I know it."

"Then why did we stop?"

"Because you are going to change shirts and hats with my brother."

"What? Why do you want to do that?"

"Because Joe has been admiring your shirt," Win said.

"You're crazy, I'm not changing shirts with your brother," Sims said. He started to get back onto his horse, but he was stopped when he heard the metallic click of Joe's pistol being cocked.

"Now, I'm just real disappointed," Joe said. "My brother promised me I could have your shirt and hat. And here you are trying to disappoint me."

"I'm just saying it don't make no sense, that's all," Sims said. Reluctantly he began peeling off his shirt, while Joe did the same.

"What about me?" Beckett asked. "Don't I get to get naked too?"

"Your turn will come," Win replied.

"My turn will come? My turn will come for what? What the hell has got into you?" Beckett asked.

"Don't worry about it," Win said. "I'll tell you what you need to know when you need to know it."

A moment later, with Sims wearing Joe's hat and shirt, he started to get back on his horse.

"No," Win said. "Ride Joe's horse for a while."

"Would you mind tellin' me just what the hell you are doin'?" Sims asked.

"Mount up," Win said. "You'll ride back here, with me. Joe, you ride up front with Beckett. I'll ride here with Sims."

"You've gone plumb loco," Sims mumbled as he mounted Joe's horse.

Remounted, the men rode through the long, narrow draw toward the bright wedge of light at the far end. The horses' hooves clattered loudly against the stone, and the echoes tumbling back to them made it sound as if an entire troop of cavalry were riding through instead of only four men.

It wasn't until the horses emerged from the other end that Sims suddenly figured out what Win was doing.

"No!" he shouted out loud. "No, don't shoot! Don't shoot!"

"Sims, what the hell's got into you?" Beckett hissed.

"Don't you see what this son of bitch has done?" Sims shouted. "He's got me wearin' his brother's duds an' ridin' his horse! Bates! Carlisle! MacGregor! Don't shoot! It's me, Kelly!"

One of the three bushwhackers stood about one-hundred yards up the trail. He could be seen from waist up, but only in silhouette against the bright sky.

"All right, Coulter," the would-be ambusher shouted. "You pulled a pretty good one on us this time. But you got a long way to go, and I don't think you're goin' to get there."

The silhouette disappeared and, a moment later, Win heard the clatter of horses being ridden at a gallop.

"You think you're so goddamned smart," Sims said. "They'll just find someplace else. And this time they won't be fooled by changing shirts and horses."

"Sims," Win said, giving the rope one more good tug. Sims let out a choking sound. "You talk too damned much."

Chapter 19

MACGREGOR LAY ON THE TOP OF THE FLAT ROCK, LOOK-ing back along the trail over which they had just come. He saw the four riders moving slowly but steadily to the North. From this distance he had no way of telling who was who, but it didn't really matter. Even if he did know, he was much too far out of range to do anything about it.

Behind him, Bates and Carlisle sat resting. Bates was chewing on the root of a grass stem. Carlisle had his boot off, examining a blister.

"You see 'em?" Bates asked.

"Yeah. They're 'bout a mile behind us."

"You figured out who is who yet?"

"No," MacGregor admitted. "Even if I did, there ain't no place we could set up a ambush between there and here. And I sure as hell don't plan to go out into the open to take him on."

"Why not? There's five of us and only two of them."

"Where do you get five?" Carlisle asked. It was the first time he had spoken, as he had been too interested in the blister on his toe.

"Well you gotta count Sims and Beckett as bein' on our side," Bates said.

"Why? What the hell can they do? They ain't even armed."

"Well, I don't know. They can do somethin'," Bates suggested. "Get in the way so he can't get off a shot or somethin'."

"They'll get in the way, all right. They'll get themselves killed and us too," Carlisle said. "If we get another chance at an ambush like before, I say we ought to do it."

"And I say we ought to just ride away," MacGregor said. "What the hell do we owe Sims and Beckett, anyway?"

"You heard what they said last night when we was at the jail visitin' them," Bates replied. "If we'd help 'em escape, they'd lead us to the money they got from the bank robbery in Braggadocio."

"Yeah, well, I heard they didn't get but a couple hundred dollars" MacGregor said.

"That ain't what they said last night," Carlisle said. "Last night they said they got away with more'n two thousand dollars, and they'd give it all to us if we'd just help them escape."

MacGregor sighed. "All right, I'm still in," he said. "But what do we do now? I know the country from here to Commerce, and we won't get another chance like the one we just had."

"Wait, I got me an idea," Bates suggested. "Maybe there is another place."

"Where?" Carlisle asked as, wincing in pain, he put his boots back on. " 'Cause what I'd like to do is kill these two sons of bitches and get it over with."

"Well, there ain't no way they goin' to get back to Commerce without goin' through Three Wells. And there ain't no way they're going through there without stoppin' for the night. We'll just get there ahead of them, and when they stop, we'll be waitin'."

"Yeah," Carlisle said, smiling broadly. "Yeah, that's a

good idea. And maybe we can have a few drinks while we wait.''

To prevent any ambush on the trail, Win and Joe changed shirts and hats with Sims and Beckett a couple more times so that anyone watching from a distance would be thoroughly confused as to who was who. By the time they approached Three Wells, however, they were back in their proper attire.

As the four men rode toward the jail, the fact that two of them were connected by noosed rope caught the attention of many of the townspeople.

"Hey! It's Beckett!" a man shouted. "The Coulter brothers is bringin' in Kansas Charley Beckett!"

"The hell you say!"

"No, it's him, big as life! Kelly Sims, too."

"I knew them boys wouldn't stay free long. Not with the reward as big as it is."

As the shouted news traveled from one to another, a crowd began to build, and the crowd followed the four horsemen down the street, running along on the boardwalk or hurrying through the dirt. Several young boys, using bent twigs as toy guns, shot at each other as they hurried alongside.

"Bang, bang! I'm Win Coulter. You're Kansas Charley Beckett, and you're dead! Bang, bang!"

"No, I'm Joe Coulter. I don't want to be Beckett. Beckett is going to hang."

"So's Kelly Sims."

"Wish they'd do it here so we could watch, don't you?"

Beckett, who couldn't help but overhear the shouted argument, stared straight ahead and licked his lips nervously.

Joe chuckled. "What's the matter, Beckett? You're looking a little peeked around the gills."

"Those kids," Beckett growled. "Somebody ought to teach them manners."

By the time they reached the jail, a smiling Sheriff Pratt was standing on the front porch.

"Well, boys, what have you brought me?"

"Sheriff, in case you've never met these august gentle-men, the ugly one here, is Kansas Charley Beckett. The weasel-looking one is Kelly Sims," Win said. "Can you keep them overnight for us?"

Joe got down first, then held the rope as Win got down. Then the two prisoners dismounted carefully.

"Be glad to keep 'em for you," Sheriff Pratt said. "Come on, you two. I got a nice, quiet cell just waitin' for you."

"Have 'em ready to go by sunup, would you, Sheriff?" Win asked. "We've got quite a ways to go with them, yet."

"They'll be ready. In the meantime, why don't you head on down to the saloon? I think Doctor Shelby, Mitch, Rank, Andy, and the others are plannin' on givin' you all you can eat and drink, I think."

"All we can eat and drink?" Joe asked, smiling. He rubbed his stomach. "Now, that's what I call a nice wel-come."

When the two boys stepped into the saloon a few minutes later, Belle was actually the first one to greet them. She slid her arm through Joe's and escorted him over to the same table where Win had played cards with Doc and the others a few days earlier. A pitcher of beer and clean glasses were already there, and no sooner did the brothers sit down, someone brought them a plate of beans.

"We got a couple of steaks cookin', too, if you want 'em," Mitch said.

"Sounds good," Joe said. "But, what are you doin' for my brother? He's probably hungry, too."

The others looked at each other then laughed. "Tell you what . . . I'll go back there and tell the cook to throw on another," Mitch said.

"And some more beans if you got any," Joe added, tak-ing a large spoonful.

In the far corner of the same saloon, Bates, Carlisle, and MacGregor sat nursing their drinks.

"Look at the way they gather around those two," MacGregor said. "You'd think it was Abraham Lincoln sittin' there."

"Maybe it is," Bates suggested.

"What are you talkin' about, maybe it is?"

Bates looked at the other two and smiled. "Well, as I recollect, Abraham Lincoln got shot, didn't he?"

MacGregor and Carlisle laughed out loud.

"Yeah," Carlisle said. "Yeah, he did at that."

"Let's drink a toast to Old Abe," Bates offered and, laughing, the other two held their glasses out and joined in the toast.

Win and Joe ate and drank their fill that evening. Then, when the plates were empty, Belle suggested to Joe that there was one more part to the welcome-back party . . . if he was interested.

Joe smiled at her. "If you're talkin' about what I think you're talkin' about, I'm interested," he said.

"What about you, Win?" Doc asked. "Want to play another game of poker?"

Win shook his head. "Doc, I thank you for the invite, I truly do. It is always nice playing cards with honest gents, and I enjoyed our game the other day. But I am beat, and we have a long way to go, yet. I think I'm going to just get the biggest bed in the quietest room in the hotel, and I'm going to sleep the sleep of the dead."

"D'ya hear that?" Bates hissed. "The son of a bitch wants to sleep like the dead."

"Well, we'll just have to see if we can help him out," Carlisle replied.

"What about the other one? The big one?" MacGregor asked.

"You ever notice how much easier it is to break one

stick at a time?" Bates asked. "We'll take care of the Coulters just like that."

MacGregor made a motion with his hands as if he were breaking a stick, then he laughed out loud.

Joe went upstairs over the saloon with Belle. But Win, opting for a quieter room, waved good-bye to the others, then walked over to the Morning Star hotel. There he got the room overlooking the street.

"Will you require a knock on your door to awaken you, Mr. Coulter?" the desk clerk asked.

"I'll probably either wake myself or my brother will come for me," Win said as he signed the guest registration book. "But if you haven't seen me by sunup, give me a yell."

"Yes, sir, Mr. Coulter, it'll be my pleasure," the hotel clerk said.

Win climbed the stairs and started down the long corridor to his room. The corridor was well-lighted with wall-mounted gas lanterns, which heated and filled the hallway with their quiet hissing. The room, though, was dark, cool, and inviting. The window was open, and a gentle night breeze lifted the gauze curtains. Win lit the lantern alongside his bed, took his gunbelt off, then stepped up to the open window and looked out onto the dark street below. From there he could see the side of the jail and the small, barred window at the cell where Sheriff Pratt had put the prisoners. He saw no one, but it was dark inside the cell so even if someone was standing at the window, he wouldn't have been able to see them. He yawned and stretched, then went over to extinguish the lamp, and the room went dark.

"There!" Bates said. "Did you see the son of a bitch standing there in his window, just as cool as you please?"

"Yeah, I saw him," Carlisle said. "You'd think he'd have better sense than to stand there like that. Why, if we'd had a rifle, we could a picked him off like shootin' a fish in a barrel.''

"And if a frog had wings he wouldn't bump his ass ever'time he jumps," Bates growled. "Come on, let's go down to the jail and have a word with Sims and Beckett."

The three men walked back to the rear of the saloon, then moved along behind the row of buildings toward the jail. As they walked, their nostrils were assailed by unpleasant odors, from stale beer, to privies, to garbage dumps of rotted food. These were, however, odors of such familiarity that they scarcely noticed.

"There it is," Bates said when they reached the rear of the barber shop.

The three men moved quickly across the narrow space between the barber shop and the jail, then stood up against the wall of the jail. There the shadows and darkness shielded them from view, even if someone had been walking down the street right in front of the jail.

"Hey!" Bates called. "Hey, Beckett! Sims! You fellas in there?"

Beckett's face appeared in the cell window. "Yeah, we're here," Beckett said. "Where've you guys been? We haven't seen you since early this mornin'."

"I know. After the Coulters pulled that trick on us, changin' shirts and hats with you, we didn't get another chance," Bates said. "Until now."

"Now? What are you goin' to do now?" Sims asked, his face joining Beckett's in the window.

"One of the Coulters is upstairs over the saloon with a whore. The other one took hisself a room over to the hotel," Carlisle explained. "Soon's we're sure the one that's in the hotel is good asleep, we're goin' to go over and take care of him."

"What about the other one?"

"Too many people in the saloon . . . too many men done gone upstairs with the whores. No way we could take care of that one quiet. That's why we're goin' after the one in the hotel.''

"Why don't you just forget about both of 'em and get us out of here?'' Beckett said.

"Not yet.''

"What do you mean 'not yet', you bastards?'' Beckett hissed. "Goddamnit, the Coulters is plannin' on takin' us back to hang! Get us out of here!''

"If we get you out before we get one of the Coulters, they'll both be comin' after us,'' MacGregor said. "We figure if they's just one of 'em left, we can handle 'im.''

"Then get us out of here and we'll help you get him,'' Beckett suggested.

"No,'' MacGregor replied, shaking his head. "Me an' Bates an' Carlisle done talked it over. If we get you out now, someone is liable to hear the commotion and we'll lose our chance at the Coulters. I'm tellin' you, right now is the best chance there's ever been to kill one of 'em.''

"All right, all right,'' Beckett agreed. "Kill the son of a bitch. Hell, I want the bastard dead more'n anyone. But don't leave us to rot here once you get the job done.''

"Don't worry, you won't be rottin' here. Once we'll be goin' after that money you promised us.''

"Yeah, don't forget the money,'' Beckett said.

"Listen, Beckett, just in case somethin' goes wrong, why don't you tell us where the money is?'' Bates suggested.

"What do you mean, in case somethin' goes wrong?''

"You know . . . if they get on to us and we have to ske-daddle. We might not get another chance this good before you two boys gets hung, and if that happens, the money won't do anyone any good, 'cause you're the only ones who know where it is.''

"Yeah,'' Carlisle said. "I think Bates has got a good point. Why don't you tell us where the money is?''

"We'll show you where the money is. We ain't goin' to tell you,'' Beckett said. "So I guess that means you are goin' to have to get us out of here.''

"All right. I was just tryin' to plan ahead, that's all," Bates said.

"When you goin' to get Coulter?"

" 'Bout midnight. Right now we're goin' to go back and have a few drinks to while away the time. Then, come twelve, we'll mosey on over to the hotel and do the job."

"Listen for the shots," Carlisle added. "When you hear the shots, you'll know it's us, takin' care of business."

Chapter 20

THE GIRL GOT UP FROM THE BED AND WALKED OVER TO A small table, where she poured water into the large porcelain basin. When she saw Carlisle staring at her, she picked up the basin and went behind the dressing screen.

"What the hell did you do that for?" Carlisle asked.

"There are some things a girl needs to do in private," she answered. There was a ripple of water as she dipped the washcloth into the basin.

"You ain't a girl, you're a whore," Carlisle said gruffly. "And since I paid for your time, there ain't none of it private. Now take down that there screen."

There was another rippling sound of water, but the screen stayed up.

"I said, take down that there screen!" Carlisle shouted, and he got out of bed and knocked the dressing screen across the room, where it hit the wall, then splintered.

The girl let out a quick shout of fear, then cringed, frightened that he was about to hit her.

"I ain't goin' to hit you," he said. "I'm just goin' to watch. Now, go on about your business."

The girl, sobbing silently in fear and embarrassment, dipped the cloth in the water and continued bathing. There was a loud knock on the door.

"Sue! Sue, you all right?" a man's voice called.

"Don't you worry none about the little girlie," Carlisle called back. "She's just fine."

"Sue?" the voice called again.

"Go on about your business, goddamnit!" Carlisle shouted. "I told you the girl is just fine."

"I want to hear her voice," the man outside the door insisted.

Carlisle walked over to his pants and pulled his pistol from his holster. He pointed it at the door and cocked it.

"I ain't a goin' to tell you no more," he said.

"No, don't!" Sue shouted. "Smokey, it's all right! I'm fine."

"You sure? I thought I heard you yell," Smokey's voice called from the other side of the door.

"It's all right, really," Sue said. "I . . . I knocked over the dressing screen by accident, that's all."

"All right," Smokey said reluctantly. "But you call me if you need me."

"Go on back to your drinkin', cowboy," Carlisle said. "And let us get back to our business." He laughed mockingly.

"I'll . . . I'll be downstairs," Smokey said.

Sue stood up.

"What are you doin'?" Carlisle asked.

"I'm finished," she said.

"You're finished? That's all there is to it?"

Sue nodded.

"Hell, what was you so private about. You didn't do nothin' but splash a little water onto yourself."

"Do you want me to bathe you?" Sue asked.

"What?" Carlisle asked, covering himself indignantly. "No! I took me a bath not no more than a week or so ago. I done it all by myself. And if and when I need another'n, why, I'll take that one by myself, too. Fact is, why'n't you just turn your back now an' let me get dressed?"

"Whatever you say," Sue said, waiting until she turned before she smiled at his sudden case of modesty.

Carlisle was still packing his shirt tail down in his pants as he came down the stairs to join Bates and MacGregor.

"How was she?" MacGregor asked.

"You want to know how she was, you spend your own money, you cheap Scot bastard," Carlisle said.

MacGregor chuckled. "Don't need to," he said. "I figure you'll pay for it, then you won't be able to keep quiet about it. Pretty soon you'll be talkin' about it so much we won't be able to get you to shut up."

"You don't say," Carlisle replied. "Well, I ain't talkin' yet. What time is it?" he asked.

Bates pointed to the clock on the wall behind the bar. "Accordin' to that it's near onto midnight," he said.

"You think he's asleep yet?"

"I reckon he is. He had a hard day and he figures to get up early for another hard day tomorrow. I reckon he's asleep by now."

"What about the one here? The one upstairs? Did you see or hear anything from him while you were up there?" Bates asked.

"My mind was otherwise occupied while I was up there," Carlisle answered.

MacGregor chuckled again. "Wasn't your mind occupied, Carlisle."

Carlisle loosened the pistol in his holster. "Come on, let's get this over with. What do you say we pay the son of a bitch a visit?"

Carlisle, Bates, and MacGregor left the saloon, then slipped quickly and quietly through the dark of night to the front of the hotel, where they stopped.

"Look around!" Bates hissed. "You see the sheriff or one of his deputies makin' rounds?"

"I don't see nobody," MacGregor replied.

"All right, let's go in."

The lobby was lighted by only one small lamp. Therefore it was fairly dark. It was deserted as well, for the chairs and sofas that were sometimes occupied by guests were all empty. Only the night clerk was in the lobby, and he was sitting in a chair behind the desk. His chair was tipped back, his head slumped forward. His chest was rising and falling in rhythm with his snores.

MacGregor started toward the desk.

"Where you goin'?" Carlisle hissed.

"To find out what room he's in," Carlisle replied.

When MacGregor reached the desk, he turned the hotel register around and ran his finger down the list of occupants. He found Win Coulter's name, written in a bold, easy-to-read signature. He hurried back to the others.

"Find 'im?" Bates asked.

"Yeah. Two-oh-two."

"Get your guns out, gents, and be quiet," Carlisle whispered, pulling out his own pistol.

With guns drawn, they slipped through the shadows of the lobby, then started up the stairs. When they reached the top, Carlisle held his finger across his lips. Here, the light was so bright they had to squint.

"Get those damned lights out!" Bates ordered, and MacGregor moved quickly down the corridor, extinguishing each lamp until the hallway was a long tunnel of darkness.

"Come on!" MacGregor hissed loudly. "That's his door down there!"

The three men moved silently through the dark hall until they were just outside the door.

"Shall we break it in?" Carlisle asked.

"I don't know," Bates replied. "If we don't get it the first time, he'll hear the commotion and we'll be sittin' ducks out here."

"How else we goin' to get in?" Carlisle wanted to know.

"Why don't we just try the doorknob?" MacGregor suggested, turning it slowly.

"You stupid or somethin'? You think he'd be crazy enough to leave it unlocked?" Carlisle asked.

The door swung open.

"Would you look at that? He didn't even lock it," Bates said, voicing the surprise of all of them.

"Go on in."

Because of the pale moonlight that fell through the open window, the room was brighter than the now-darkened hallway. They could see the bed and Win's hat and pistol belt hanging from the brass bedpost.

"This is goin' to be like takin' candy from a baby," Bates said, aiming at the bed.

Bates fired and his shot was followed almost immediately by the other two so that, for a moment, all three guns were firing, lighting up the darkness with white flashes and filling the room with thunder.

After firing three shots apiece, Bates shouted to stop firing.

"The whole town will be in here in a minute. We got to get out of here," he said. "Check and make sure the son of a bitch is dead!"

MacGregor walked over to the bed and felt around, then gasped in surprise.

"Bates! He ain't here!" he shouted.

"What? Where is he?"

"I'm right here," Win said. He was standing on the porch roof, just outside his window.

With shouts of frustrated rage and fear, all three would-be assassins turned their guns toward the window and began firing. Bullets crashed through the window, sending large shards of glass out onto the porch roof. Win had jumped to one side of the window as soon as he spoke, and thus avoided the initial fusillade. After the first volley, Win leaned around and fired into the room. He hit one of the men and saw him go down. The other two bolted through the door.

At first Win planned to go after them by climbing back

into the room, but he knew they would be leaving the hotel, so he decided to just wait until they were on the street. There, they would have fewer places to hide . . . and there would be less likelihood of an innocent bystander being hurt.

Win, who had been sleeping on the porch roof, fully clothed, ran to the edge of the roof, then jumped down into the space between the hotel and the building next door. He waited there in the shadows and kept his eyes on the front door of the hotel. As he expected, the door burst open a moment later and two men ran out. Win stepped out into the street to brace them.

"Hold it right there!" he called to them.

"It's Coulter!" one of the two men shouted, and he fired.

The bullet whizzed by Win's ear, much closer than was comfortable, and Win returned fire, shooting above, and just to the right of the shooter's flame pattern. He heard a grunt of pain.

The lone survivor darted across the street and disappeared into the darkness on the other side. Crouching low, Win moved back into the darkness on his side of the street, then began searching, trying to find his quarry. He saw Joe coming out of the front door of the saloon.

"Joe, get out of the light!" Win called.

Joe moved into the shadows, then ran across the street. He squatted down beside Win. "What's goin' on?" he asked. "Did Beckett and Sims escape?"

"No," Win said. "But the three men who were trailing us paid me a visit."

The assailant fired from the shadows on the other side of the street, and his bullet hit the post between Joe and Win, sending pieces of wooden splinters into their faces.

"Damn, that hurt!" Joe said, pulling a splinter from his cheek.

"How'd the son of a bitch see us here?" Win asked.

"There," Joe said, pointing.

Someone in the building behind them, curious as to what

was going on, had lit a lantern. It sent a golden splash of light outside, putting Win and Joe in silhouette.

"Shoot through the window," Win said. "That'll make them extinguish the lantern. But don't hit anyone."

Joe nodded, then sent a bullet through the window in the corner. It had the desired effect, for the lantern went out immediately.

As soon as Joe shot, they changed locations, which was good because, from the shadows on the other side of the road, their assailant fired at them, using the flame pattern of Joe's shot as his target.

Win shot back at the assailant's flame pattern, but he knew it was a wasted shot. The guy was pretty good, and knew to move after each shot.

Suddenly a horse burst out of the shadows from across the street, and its rider, bending low, began firing at Win and Joe.

Both Joe and Win fired back. They missed the rider, but one of them hit a lit kerosene lantern than hung on an arm sticking out over the street from the corner of the leather goods store. The bullet burst the kerosene tank and sent the fuel up into the lighted chimney, causing the lantern to explode. When it did so, it sent a shower of flaming kerosene onto the rider's back.

"Ahhhhiieee!" the rider screamed in terror and pain as he galloped down the street, flaming now like a human torch.

Win stepped out into the street and held his pistol out in front of him. He took a long, careful aim at the ball of fire, which had now panicked his horse into galloping faster than ever. By now the outlaw was nearly one-hundred yards away.

Win squeezed the trigger and the pistol fired. At the far end of the street, the fleeing, flaming, rider pitched out of his saddle with a bullet in the back of his head, dead before he even hit the dirt. He lay there on the ground, burning for several seconds until a couple of the citizens from that

end of town, having been awakened by the commotion,
hurried out into the street to douse the flames.

By now Sheriff Pratt was on the scene, wearing pants,
boots, and his undershirt. He hadn't even bothered to strap
on his pistol, though he was carrying a rifle.

"What happened?" he asked.

"Some men tried to kill me," Win explained. "There's
one up in my hotel room, and another across the street."
He pointed to a body, close by in the street. That body,
like the one at the far end of the street, was already drawing
a crowd.

"Are they locals?" the sheriff asked in surprise.

Win shook his head. "I don't think so. I think these were
the same men we saw dogging us on the trail today. I was
pretty sure they might try again tonight, so I was ready for
them."

Sheriff Pratt shook his head and chuckled. "Ready for
them, huh? I guess you were."

Chapter 21

THREE WELLS HAD TELEGRAPHED AHEAD THE NEWS THAT Win and Joe Coulter would be arriving with Kelly Sims and Kansas Charley Beckett. So when the three men rode into Commerce, the entire town was turned out to meet them.

"Did they give you boys much of a fight?" someone called.

"Hey, Kansas Charley, you think you'll get away this time?"

"I'll be comin' to your dance, Beckett!"

Beckett stared ahead glumly, and when they reached the jail, Sheriff McQuade and Judge Smiley were standing there on the porch to meet them.

"Well, Beckett, I've been wanting to have you as my guest for a long, long time," Sheriff McQuade said.

"You go to hell," Beckett snarled.

"Now, that's no way to be," McQuade said.

"I hope you got somethin' to eat in there," Sims said. "We ain't et nothin' but jerky for three days, now." Sims started toward the front door of the jailhouse, but Sheriff McQuade reached out his hand to stop him.

"Huh uh, Charley, you won't be goin' in there," he said.

"What do you mean?"

"Boys, take him over to the courtyard and put him in the holding cell."

"The holding cell?" Sims said in dread. "No! What are you goin' to put me there for?"

"Why, Mr. Sims, don't you remember?" McQuade said. "That's where you were headed when you escaped."

"Yeah, but you don't go there until just before you hang. What is this, a lynchin'? Don't I even get a trial first?"

"You've had your trial," Judge Smiley replied. "There's no need to try you again. You were found guilty, you were sentenced to hang, and hang you shall, this very afternoon."

"No! Beckett, do somethin'," Sims shouted as a couple of deputies led him toward the courthouse. "They're fixin' to hang me!"

"Quit your belly achin', Sims, an' take your hanging like a man," Beckett said.

"Is that all you got to say?" Sims asked.

"Ain't my problem," Beckett said. "I ain't the one hanging this afternoon. You are."

"You son of bitch! I'll see you in hell!" Sims shouted as they took him away.

Beckett began to laugh.

"I don't know what you have to laugh about, Beckett," Sheriff McQuade said. "I figure we'll have you tried tomorrow mornin' and hung by tomorrow afternoon."

"Yeah? Well, I ain't got no rope around my neck yet. And you can ask these here Missouri pukes, I ain't that easy to hold on to. Tell him, Coulter. Tell him!" Beckett said, with a mocking laugh.

"Beckett, I'm going to enjoy watching you hang. And if the sheriff's arm is sore, I'll even pull the handle myself," Win said.

"I'll have the money ready for you two boys this afternoon," Judge Smiley said.

"Money?" Beckett said. He looked at Win and Joe. "I

thought this was something personal between us, something from the war. Didn't know you was gettin' blood money.''

"It is personal," Joe said. "And knowing it's money for your blood makes it even sweeter."

"We'll be around this afternoon, Judge," Win said. "But first we're going to take a bath, get a good, hot meal, then a hotel room. If we're going to wait around to see Beckett hang, we may as well wait in comfort."

"You son of a bitch! You'll never see me hang!" Beckett said.

"Get him inside," Judge Smiley ordered, and Sheriff McQuade and the remaining deputy escorted Beckett into the jail.

By two o'clock in the afternoon, both Coulters were bathed, wearing clean clothes, and standing in Judge Smiley's office.

"I've got the money right here for you boys," Judge Smiley said, taking it out of his desk drawer. "The reward I promised you for Beckett plus the reward that was already posted for the others. And I must tell you, I have never paid out a reward with more pleasure. That is one bunch of men I am glad to see gone. He counted the money, then held it out. "Who gets it?"

"Give it to Joe," Win said. "He's the one that keeps up with our money."

"Thanks," Joe said, taking the money. "What time will Beckett's trial be tomorrow?"

"Nine in the morning," Judge Smiley answered. "We'll find him guilty by eleven, feed him his last meal at twelve, and hang him at two."

"We'll be there."

Judge Smiley stroked his chin. "You know, you got paid the same for all of them. But I get the distinct feeling you got more satisfaction from bringing him in than all the others put together."

"That's right," Win said.

"Why? Because of the girl? You knew her, didn't you?"

"Yes. We knew her. Her mother is a relative of ours, and her father once rode with us."

"Rode with you? Oh, you mean during the war?"

"Yes."

"Wait a minute, Beckett was a Jayhawker, wasn't he? And you boys were with Quantrill, I believe? Yes, I can see where there might be bad blood between you."

"The bad blood started even before we joined Quantrill," Joe said.

"Oh? How can that be?"

Joe told about finding their house burned and their parents murdered.

"The head of that band of murdering bastards was a man named Emil Slaughter. And what they did had nothing to do with the war."

The sheriff nodded toward the back of the jail. "And Beckett? What was his role in that?"

"Beckett rode with Slaughter. That's enough," Joe said.

"I see. Then that would make it worse. Well, I not only congratulate you boys for bringing him in, I commend you for not letting your personal feelings get in the way. I know you were tempted to kill Beckett yourself, and, under the circumstances, if you had done it, you would probably have gotten away with it. I admire your respect for the law."

Win smiled. "Respect for the law has nothing to do with it," he said. "I never met anyone yet who wouldn't rather be shot than hung."

There was a knock on the door and Judge Smiley yelled for whoever it was to come in. It was his law clerk.

"Judge," the clerk said. "They've got Kelly Sims standing out on the gallows. The sheriff is waiting for your signal."

"Yes," Judge Smiley said. He sighed and looked up at Win. "You know I can sentence someone to die, and in the case of a person like Kelly Sims, a cold blooded murderer, I can do it with a clear conscience. But when it comes to the part where I actually have to give the signal to dispatch the soul of another human being into eternity, I must confess to having qualms." He walked over to the window. "Come, watch with me," he said. "After all, you have a hand in this, too."

Win and Joe walked over to the window and looked down into the courtyard below. There were three or four-hundred people gathered around the gallows. There were reporters and a photographer in the front row. Although Sims had just been brought in that same morning, the reporters were local only, there being insufficient time to gather any from the national newspapers.

Sims was standing just under the crossbeam with the noose around his neck and a hood over his face. His hands were manacled to his belt, so that his arms were stiffly by his sides. His legs were tied together. Any last words he may have had were already spoken at that point, and he was quietly counting off the last seconds of his life.

Judge Smiley nodded his head, and down on the gallows, Sheriff McQuade, who had been awaiting the signal, pulled the handle. From his position at the open window in Judge Smiley's office, Win and Joe could hear the thump of the dropping trapdoor, then the oohs and aahs of the assembled crowd. Kelly Sims dropped straight and true, made one half turn to the left, then was very still.

Though the sun was a full disk up in the Eastern sky, Win was still sound asleep. He was awakened by a loud banging on his hotel room door. He sat up quickly, drawing his gun from the holster, which hung on the bedstead.

"What is it?" he shouted gruffly.

"Coulter, it's me, Sheriff McQuade. Open up."

Still holding his gun, Win walked over to the door and opened it slightly, just to make certain the sheriff was alone. When he saw that he was alone, he opened it all the way.

"Yeah, come on in," he said invitingly. He took his pants off the back of the chair and started putting them on.

As he did so, he saw the look of agitation on the sheriff's face. "Is it Beckett?" he asked.

"Yes. How did you know?"

"Just a hunch."

"When I came to the office this morning, I found my night deputy lying dead, just outside the cell. His throat had been cut. Evidently Beckett had lured him over to the cell on some pretense, then managed to cut his throat and get the keys."

Joe came out into the hallway from the room next door, still tucking his shirt into his trousers. "You say the deputy's throat was cut?" Joe asked.

"Yes. He bled to death on the floor of the jail. My God, you should see the blood."

"How did Beckett get a knife?" Joe asked. "I know for a fact, he didn't have one when we brought him in."

"Well, that's the damndest thing," McQuade said. "He took a piece from the bed and made himself a knife."

"You seem to have a hell of a time holding on to your prisoners, Sheriff," Win challenged.

"I can't deny that," the sheriff said contritely.

"Have you looked around your office? What's missing?" Win asked.

"A rifle, pistol and holster, and two or three boxes of ammunition. It looks like he also took the deputy's horse, so he's well armed and well mounted."

By now Win had on his boots and was strapping on his gun. "So are we," he said.

"Then you boys are going after him? That's a relief, I was hoping you would be. You'll bring him back?"

"You asked two questions, Sheriff," Win replied. "And I'm only going to answer the first one. Yes, we are going after him."

Chapter 22

THE COULTERS WERE ABLE TO FOLLOW BECKETT BECAUSE the deputy's horse he was riding was a town horse. As a town horse, his food consisted primarily of oats. That made his droppings very distinctive.

Joe, who was the better tracker of the two, was dismounted, reading a sign. Win, who was still in the saddle, took a swallow of water from his canteen, ran the back of his hand across his lips, then replaced the canteen.

"What do you think, little brother?" he asked.

Joe stood up, then looked toward the South. "You know, at first I thought Beckett would be heading for Aquilla, but I think he has something else in mind."

"What?"

"I think he's heading for Mexico."

"Damn," Win said. "And he's got what? A three-hour head start on us?"

"Doesn't matter," Joe said. "The way he's pushing, he'll kill his horse long before he reaches the border."

Though it was difficult to keep themselves in check, Win and Joe rode easily, sparingly, knowing that in the long run they would make just as good time because their animals would still be fresh, while Beckett's horse would be wearing out.

On the third day, they got close enough to get a glimpse of Beckett in the distance. That was when they knew he was heading for Sorento, another one of the little towns on the American side of the border.

The boys arrived in Sorento at just about supper time, and, along with the spicy aromas of Mexican cooking, they could smell coffee, pork chops, fried potatoes, and baking bread.

"Sasha? Sasha?" a woman called, and Joe, startled because the woman was very close to him, jerked his horse to a halt to look in the direction of the call.

"Si, Signora?" A young Mexican girl answered.

"Take the clothes down from the line, will you?" the woman ordered.

"Si, Signora," the servant girl replied.

The woman looked at Joe nervously and took a step backwards. Joe touched the brim of his hat in greeting, then urged his horse on.

In front of the feed store, two gray-bearded men were engaged in a game of checkers, watched over by a half-dozen kibitzers. A couple of them looked up as Win and Joe rode by, their horses' hooves clattering loudly on the hard-packed street. Neither of the kibitzers seemed to recognize them. That was good, because they didn't exactly want their presence announced.

The shopkeeper of the dry goods store stepped through his front door and began vigorously sweeping the wooden porch. His broom did little but cause the dust to swirl about, then fall back down again. He brushed a sleeping dog off the porch, but even before the shopkeeper was back inside, the dog reclaimed his position, curled around comfortably, and, within a moment was asleep again.

Joe saw the horse from the far end of the street. As he had known from the trail, the horse had been ridden nearly to death, and even from there he could see that the animal was totally defeated.

"There's his horse," Joe said, pointing to the horse.

"Anyone who would treat an animal like that should be horsewhipped."

The two brothers rode slowly down to the far end of the street, then tied their horses to a hitch rail next to the poor animal. Joe walked over to the horse and patted it on the neck. The horse's coat was smeared with foam and it was breathing in labored gasps. Its muzzle and the hitch rail were flecked with blood, which had spewed from its mouth and nostrils by the painful breaths.

"Oh, Jesus," Joe said. He looked at Win with an expression of sorrow and outrage on his face. "Look at the blood. The poor critter's lungs have burst."

"What can be done for it?" Win asked.

Joe shook his head. "Nothing. He's in unbearable pain." Sighing, Joe pulled his pistol and aimed it at the horse's head. The horse looked toward him, his big brown eyes sad and knowing. He nodded once, almost as if telling Joe that he understood what had to be done. The horse looked away then and waited stoically for the release from its suffering. Joe pulled the trigger and the horse fell to the ground. The gunshot echoed through the quiet streets for a long time. Then it was silent.

The gunshot attracted several of the townspeople, and they looked toward the saloon at the two men, one with a smoking gun, and at the horse lying motionless on the street. A curtain fluttered in one of the false fronts. A cat yowled somewhere down the street. A fly buzzed past Joe's ear, did a few circles, then descended quickly to the horse, joined almost immediately by a dozen others, drawn to the unexpected feast.

Leaving Joe out front, Win pushed through the bat-wing doors, then stepped to one side, with a wall at his back. At the bar, a glass of beer in front of him, his lips dripping with moisture, stood Kansas Charley Beckett.

Win's lips twisted into an evil smile. Part of him wanted to kill the man that instant, while part of him wanted to delay his pleasure. He remembered the fear Kelly Sims had shown toward hanging, and he wanted Beckett to know that same terror. Maybe he would take him back.

"Beckett," Win said. His words were cold, flat, menacing.

Beckett didn't turn around, didn't even look at him in the mirror. Instead, he stared into his glass of beer with those cold, droopy eyes.

"Well, look who is here. I would've thought you'd give up on me by now."

"I've come for you, Beckett."

There were a half-dozen drinkers at the bar, and at Win's words, they hurried to get away. Tables and chairs scooted across the floor as everyone in the saloon got up and moved back against the wall, out of the line of fire.

Win caught the movement of the others out of the corner of his eye. He was pretty sure Beckett had not picked up any partners in his short flight of freedom, but he wanted to be certain. A quick glance was all it took to convince him that there was no one else who represented any danger to him.

Beckett still did not turn around. "What was that shooting out front?" he asked.

"My brother shot your horse."

"He shouldn't have done that. That was a good horse."

"Not after you got through with him, you horse-killing son of a bitch. You rode him until his lungs burst."

"Son of a bitch, did you hear that?" one of the saloon patrons asked.

"That's no way to treat a horse," another said.

Beckett paid no attention to the comments. "Well, he wasn't my horse, anyway," Beckett said. "As you know, I just borrowed him when I left," Beckett said with a low, evil laugh.

"You disappointed a few folks back there, Beckett. They were wanting to see you dance."

"Did I? Well, I thought I'd just let Mr. Sims do the dancing for both of us."

"Sims did his show. Now it's your turn."

"No thank you. I got no plans to go hang."

"I don't give a damn what your plans are, Beckett. You're going back, and you're going to hang."

"If you're so all fired set on seein' me dead, Beckett, why don't you just shoot me here and be done with it?"

"No way" Win said. "Shooting is too good for you. I saw the way Sims sweated before he was hung. I don't intend to deny myself the pleasure of seeing you go through the same thing."

Beckett turned away from the bar to look at Win. He was smiling evilly.

"You know, Coulter, I wondered why you and your brother was doggin' me like you been doin'. Then someone told me that you took it real personal what me and Mendoza did to that young Pemberton girl." He rubbed himself. "She was young, but she was fine. Just real fine."

A blood vessel in Win's temple began to work, and his eyes narrowed.

Seeing that his words were having some effect on him, Beckett continued. "They said you was some kin to her. Is that right?"

"That's right," Win said.

"That why you and your brother dogged me so hard?"

"That's why."

Beckett's evil smile spread. "Well, then maybe I got somethin' here that'll square things up between us. Somethin' that belonged to that little ol' girl. If you want, you can keep it as a little memento." He started to reach into his vest pocket.

"Don't do it, Beckett!" Win cautioned.

Beckett held out his hand. "Hey, now, hold on there," he said. "I ain't goin' for no gun. Like I told you, all I'm reachin' for is a little memento." His hand came back out of his pocket, clutching a little piece of brown leather. "See?" He held it out toward Win. "This here is for you. You and your brother. I'm givin' it to you."

"What is it?" Win asked, trying to study it from where he stood.

Beckett's evil grin grew wider. "Hell, I thought you said you knowed her, Coulter. What's the matter? Didn't you ever see the girl's titties? This here is one of her titties. The left one."

Suddenly a picture flashed in Win's mind. He could recall vividly the scene of her mutilated body and the missing left breast. He realized at that moment that Beckett was telling the truth.

"You sorry son of a bitch," he swore.

"Here, take it!" Beckett suddenly shouted, tossing it toward Win.

Win's first reaction was of revulsion, then he saw that Beckett was using that as a diversionary tactic, for in the same motion of the toss, his hand snaked down to his side to draw his pistol.

Win reacted to the sudden move quickly, drawing his own pistol faster than he had ever drawn it before, spurred on in the effort by years of controlled rage toward this man, the rage highlighted by his latest atrocity. He had his own gun out in time to take quick but deliberate aim and shoot Beckett in the gut. Beckett, the barrel of his own pistol just topping the holster, pulled the trigger, shooting lead into the floor. A red stain began to spread just over his belt buckle.

Beckett's gun clattered to the floor, and he put his hands over his belly wound and watched the blood spill through his fingers. Inexplicably, he smiled.

"You're fast, Coulter," he said. "Faster'n I thought." He weaved back and forth for a moment, then pitched forward, crashing through a table before landing on the floor.

Smoke from the discharge of the two weapons formed a big cloud, then began to drift toward the ceiling.

"Win!" Joe shouted, coming inside at the sound of the gunshots.

"I'm all right, little brother," Win answered, holding his

hand out toward Joe. Joe, who had drawn his pistol, looked down at Beckett. Seeing that Beckett represented no danger to either of them, Joe put his gun away.

Win knelt beside Beckett. Beckett, who was still alive, struggled to sit up. Win helped him, then leaned him back against the bar. Beckett looked at Win and smiled. As he did so, a trickle of blood ran from his mouth . . . evidence that the bullet had pierced his lung. Every breath was painful to him, and it was evident in his face as he breathed.

"Well, I reckon you've killed me," he said.

"This isn't how I wanted you to die, Beckett," Win replied. "I wanted to take you back. I wanted to see you hang."

Beckett tried to laugh, but it came out in a barking cough. Little flecks of blood sprayed out on his lips and on his shirt.

"When you think about it, I reckon I beat you after all," he rasped. "I told you I wasn't goin' to hang, and as you can see, I ain't."

"I guess you're right," Win said. He stood up and rammed his pistol back in his holster. "But dead's dead, I reckon."

The bat-wing doors swung open and a man with a badge came inside. His hair and mustache were gray, his face lined around his blue eyes. There was a sharpness to his eyes that told Win the peace officer had probably been pretty good when he was younger. Only age had driven him to a backwater place like Sorento, where little happened. Age had undoubtedly slowed him down, but Win imagined there were still a few who could make the mistake of misjudging him. Win didn't intend to make that mistake.

"You shoot this fella?" the man with the badge asked, nodding toward Beckett, who was leaning back against the bar.

"Yes," Win answered.

"Want to tell me what it's all about?"

Beckett tried to laugh, another coughing, blood-spraying

laugh. "Sheriff, don't blame my friend here," he said. "If he hadn't killed me, I would have killed him. Fact is, he done me a favor. This way, at least, I ain't going to hang."

"That's right, Sheriff," one of the witnesses said. "The fella on the floor drew first. It was a pure case of self-defense."

"You shoulda seen it, Sheriff," another offered. "It was the fastest thing I ever seen in my life."

They looked at Win, then at Joe. "Are you two together?"

"We're brothers," Joe said.

"Did you team up on this man?"

"We tracked him here," Win said. "But when the shooting came, it was just Beckett and me."

"Beckett?" the sheriff asked in surprise, looking down at the man against the bar.

"Kansas Charley Beckett," Win said.

"I'll be damned."

"You heard of me, Sheriff?" Beckett choked. "You read any of the novels about me?"

"I've heard about you," the sheriff replied. "But what I read about you ain't been novels."

"I'm famous," Beckett said. "People in New York City have read about my exploits," he added.

"Did you have to bring your beef to my town?" the sheriff asked Win.

"Sorry, Sheriff, but this is where we caught up with him," Win replied.

"You two boys bounty hunters?"

"Not really," Win said. "Though we intend to claim the reward on his miserable hide."

"Why, Sheriff, I can't believe you don't know who these men are," Beckett said. "These here boys are called the Bushwhackers."

The crowd reacted audibly to Beckett's announcement.

"The Bushwhackers?" someone said.

"The Coulters, Win and Joe," another said.

"I've heard of them."

"Boys we're goin' to have some story to tell. We just seen the Bushwhackers in action," another said.

The sheriff held up his hand to still the crowd reaction.

"I've heard of you, boys," he said. "Far as I know, you aren't wanted men, but they say you're a couple of hard cases. I've never heard-tell of either one of you killing anyone who didn't need killing. But if there's anything I don't want in this town it's a couple of gunfighters, even if there's no paper out on you. Do you get my drift?"

"We'll be on our way, Sheriff, soon as you give us a receipt that says we turned Beckett over to you."

The sheriff went over to the bar. "Ed, you got a tablet and pencil?"

The bartender reached under the bar then came up with the items.

"You really are Charles Beckett, like he says?" the sheriff asked Beckett.

"That's it, Sheriff. Charles Beckett, with two t's," Beckett said. "I don't want my name misspelled when they write the story."

"Received of Win and Joe Coulter, the body of one Charles Beckett, wanted man, killed in a fair gunfight in the town of Sorento. Signed, Sheriff Emil Dobbins," the sheriff said, speaking aloud as he wrote.

Beckett laughed weakly.

"What are you laughing at, Beckett?"

"The way you're givin' a receipt for me . . . sayin' I was killed in a gunfight, when I ain't even dead yet."

"You're dead, Beckett," the sheriff said easily. "You just ain't laid down yet." He tore the page off the tablet and handed it to Win. "Will this do for you?" he asked.

"That will do just fine, Sheriff. Thank you," Win answered, folding the piece of paper and putting it in his shirt pocket. "Come on, Joe. Let's go."

The two men started toward the door.

"Coulter, wait a minute!" Beckett called to Win. "You ain't goin' to just leave me like this, are you? I got a pain in my gut somethin' awful. Why didn't you shoot me in the head or the heart and get it over with?"

"I shot you just where I wanted to shoot you, Beckett," Win said.

"Well finish me off now, you bastard!" Beckett shouted. "Don't you leave me like this!"

Win started for the door again.

"Coulter! Coulter! Don't forget the girl's tit!" Beckett called. "You wouldn't want to leave her tittie behind for someone else to play with, would you?"

Win stopped.

"Yeah!" Beckett said, seeing Win weaken. "Yeah, think about that little tittie. I cut it offen her, Coulter. And she wasn't dead yet, neither. She screamed like a stuck pig when I cut it offen her."

Win remained rooted to the floor, though his hand began to move slowly toward his pistol.

"That's it!" Beckett said. "That's it! Shoot me! Yes, go ahead! Shoot me!"

Win sighed and let his arm drop down to his side. He started once more toward the door.

"Don't you want me to die? What's the matter? Are you showing yellow?"

Win and Joe pushed through the bat-wing doors, walked by Beckett's dead horse, then climbed on their own horses for the long ride back to Commerce. Behind them, they could hear Beckett's screams of rage and pain. It was like music to their ears.